THE
WRONG SORT
OF STORIES

THE WRONG SORT OF STORIES

Stephen Measure

Silver Layer Publications

Silver Layer Publications
P.O. Box 1047
Chino Valley, AZ 86323
www.silverlayer.com
www.stephenmeasure.com

Proofreading: Angela Carter
Cover illustration: Brian Raty
Cover design: Heidi Ross
Book design: Marny K. Parkin

Library of Congress Control Number: 2015947908

ISBN: 978-1-940778-32-7 (hardback)
ISBN: 978-1-940778-30-3 (paperback)

Last Updated: June 14, 2017 (copyright page)

Contents

It needs to be said.
I can say it.
Therefore, I should.

The Unneeded Panic Room

MICHAEL WAS A DENTIST, A FATHER OF two, and a happy man married to a beautiful wife. He lit fireworks on the Fourth of July, swapped lost teeth under his kids' pillows for loose change, and fried a mean turkey on Thanksgiving Day. He drove a small hybrid SUV, washed the dishes since his wife cooked, and enjoyed sci-fi marathons. All in all, he was a fairly ordinary man. He was religious, sure—Mormon to be exact—and that made him a bit peculiar, but what could be more ordinary than to be a bit peculiar? His opinions were average. Were they even his own? How could he know, when they matched so seamlessly with the rest of the crowd?

But then one day they didn't. He was still a dentist, a father, a lucky husband. He still lit fireworks, traded teeth for cash, and fried turkeys. The SUV was still there, the dishes were still washed, the sci-fi shows still watched. So much was the same, yet so much was different. The world had shifted. The crowd had chosen a new opinion. It had stepped to one side, yet Michael didn't follow. He stayed where he'd always been. Michael didn't move.

Months earlier, Michael was wrapping up a grueling day in his dental office. As an introvert, he was often worn out by the interactions he had with people throughout the day, but today had been more stressful than most. One of his patients had had the unfortunate luck of meeting the metal bar of his trampoline. More specifically, his front teeth had had the unfortunate luck—all of them. Michael had taken a picture on his cell phone, which he intended to save for the day his daughter, Grizzy, ever asked to get a trampoline.

"Dad, I want a trampoline," she would undoubtedly ask one day.

"Would you rather have a trampoline, or would you rather have your front teeth?" he would say, showing her the picture.

Then again, maybe I shouldn't show Grizzy that picture, Michael thought, reminding himself about how anxious she had been lately. It was hard to understand how an eight-year-old could be so stressed. She worried about things that he didn't even know needed to be worried about—and he himself was a worrier! So, no, maybe he wouldn't be showing Grizzy that picture, not anytime soon anyway, not until she had gotten over whatever stage this was she was going through.

Michael sat at his desk in front of his computer and clicked on a hidden bookmark, bringing up a picture of some golf clubs he had been dreaming about. The price tag was fairly hefty, over a thousand dollars. But they'd almost gotten enough in their spare funds account for him to be able to swing it.

"Are you looking up your cruise again?" Rick called from his post at the front desk, seeing Michael sitting in front of his computer. Michael and his wife, Kate, were scheduled for a week-long cruise through the Caribbean next month.

"Something like that," Michael answered, closing the web browser.

"Are you looking at those golf clubs again?" Rick asked. "You know Kate will never let you buy them."

That might be true. Kate ruled the family budget with precision, always worrying about saving. Saving, saving, saving. There would be college for Grizzy, maybe a church mission, definitely a wedding. So much to save for. And they were already saving for Tank, too. He was only three, but Kate had already setup a fund she called his "Dental School Fund." She seemed to think that since he was named after his father, he was destined to follow in his father's footsteps. Michael, however, was skeptical. He thought it should be Tank's "Circus School Fund" because Tank, who at three years old already weighed more than his eight-year-old sister, was destined to be the strong man in a circus sideshow. Tank wasn't so much fat as he was just thick. Michael didn't know where it came from. Kate still fussed over a bit of baby fat, but they were both otherwise fairly skinny. Grizzy was thin, too. So what had happened with Tank?

But life was about more than just saving for your kid's future. Life was also about making your husband happy, or at least Michael was sure he could convince Kate of that fact, which would lead to his new golf clubs and perhaps a chance to go golfing later this month, or at least this year.

Michael's cell phone buzzed with a new text message from Kate.

"Call me!"

Oh, no, Michael thought, immediately worrying it was about Grizzy. She'd started getting fussy with her school lunch recently, claiming to be worried about it being poisonous or making her throw up or something. And she wasn't eating enough at home to make up for it. Their thin girl was getting thinner. If only there were some way to transfer weight from brother to sister, Michael said to himself before calling his wife on his cell phone.

"What's up?" he asked her.

Kate didn't answer for a moment. It sounded like she was finishing a drink. At least she wasn't crying, so the news wasn't horrible.

"We've got a meeting with the stake president tonight," she finally said after gulping down whatever she had been drinking.

"What? You're kidding."

"Nope. The stake executive secretary just called. They want us there at eight o'clock."

"Both of us?"

"Yup."

"Crap."

"Yup."

You see, Mormons don't have a paid clergy. Their local congregations, called wards, are led by a bishop and his counselors, all volunteers. Within the ward are the women's organization, the Relief Society; the children's organization, the Primary; and organizations for the men and for teenage boys and girls, Elders Quorum and Mutual. Each of these organizations are staffed by members in many different positions to keep things running. They're all volunteer positions, or to put it a better way: they're all *volunteered* positions. Mormons are asked to serve in a particular position, and they usually say yes. They serve there for a year or perhaps a few years, and then they are released and replaced by someone else, and they go on to another position. It was all rather routine for lifelong Mormons like Michael and Kate, who had cycled through countless positions: Sunday School teacher, Primary teacher, secretary of this and of that, but nothing big or truly demanding, and that is what had Michael worried. You see, a stake president is in charge of a handful of wards, referred to as a stake, and many of the big, demanding ward positions are assigned by him, callings like that of a bishop, or a bishop's counselor, the type of callings that Michael most definitely did not want.

Michael worried over the problem all the way home and through dinner. He thought he had had it all worked out. Mormons are a conservative bunch. When going to church, they wear church clothes: dresses or skirts for women (although, yes, nice pants are fine, too), dress shirts and ties for the men. The dress shirts are usually white, and the men in ward leadership positions usually wear suits. So Michael had a good solution to avoid any of the demanding callings: he wore a blue dress shirt to church. It was ideal—he didn't look too out of place, but he also didn't look like a leader. And his strategy had carried him from Sunday School teacher to Primary teacher to Young Men's adviser and around and around and around.

Some men seek high callings. Some women long to have their husbands thought of with such respect. But all of those people are crazy. Bishops spend ten to thirty hours a week caring for the needs of their ward, ten to thirty hours—if not more!—on top of their day jobs and their families and their hobbies. Hobbies, what are those? Anyone who wants to be a bishop is crazy. Anyone who wants to be a bishop's wife is crazy. But Michael wasn't crazy, so Michael wore his blue shirt and tie to church and everything was good and working just fine. So why in the world was the stake president calling him into his office tonight?

"Don't they know I'm not leadership material?" he asked Kate as he washed the dishes.

"Anyone that talks to you knows that," she said. "Maybe it's not about a calling. Maybe it's about something else."

"Yeah, what else?"

"I don't know."

"We have a big ward. We have lots of active men. They shouldn't need to dig into the second tier for someone like me."

"Not all stake-issued callings are that horrible though. Don't they call clerks and things like that? That wouldn't be so bad."

"Yeah," Michael said. "I guess you're right." But he couldn't get the image of the boy's missing teeth from his mind. The metal bar of the trampoline was like a high-profile calling, and he had just lost his balance and was heading straight for it.

In desperation, Michael decided on a last-ditch plan. Maybe they just don't realize how unqualified I am, he told himself. Maybe I just need to make it obvious how unsuited I am for a serious position. He decided that the best way to make this clear would be to show up in a T-shirt and jeans to the meeting that night. The stake president would undoubtedly be in a suit. If he had been inspired to give Michael a big calling, then perhaps having Michael show up in a T-shirt would inspire him to change his mind. Michael even considered wearing one of his paint shirts, but that would be pushing it too far. So he threw on one of his average T-shirts instead. Just a green shirt, no picture or anything. And he was feeling pretty good about himself and his chances until his wife walked in.

"You are *not* wearing that tonight," she said.

"Why not?"

"We're meeting with the stake president! Show some respect. Put on your shirt and tie."

Kate pulled a red-and-white striped church dress out of her closet. Michael griped as he took off his T-shirt. Then he had a brilliant idea.

"Hey," he said. "How do you know the calling is for me? Maybe they're going to give you a stake calling. Maybe they'll call you as the stake Relief Society president. Or maybe something in the stake Primary presidency."

Kate glared at him. Then she looked down at her dress and thought for a moment before putting it back in the closet and selecting a denim skirt and matching blouse to wear instead. Michael relented and switched to his blue dress shirt and church slacks. But I'm not wearing a tie! he insisted to himself. Michael and Kate were active, believing Mormons. They would accept any calling that was extended to them. But they also knew better than to invite trouble.

The car ride was a quiet one, both of them lost in their own worries about what this meeting could mean, and it didn't get any better when they were ushered into the office of their stake president, President Hart, and greeted by him with his characteristic firm handshake. Michael always worried around President Hart. The man was tall and athletic, a lawyer with a presence that filled up the room. In addition, he was black, which always made Michael incredibly self-conscious whenever they spoke. Michael admired President Hart, but Michael had been raised in a small town in the middle of Idaho and had never spoken with a black man until he went to college. This lack of experience left him constantly worried that he might somehow say or do something offensive. And then he worried that his worrying might make it more likely that he might say or do something offensive. And on, and on, and on.

That wasn't the way it was supposed to be. Michael was happy for Grizzy. The great thing about raising her in California was that her classmates had a good mix of physical characteristics. She would grow up seeing skin color the way that Michael saw hair color, as just one more physical characteristic in a long list of physical characteristics, none of them significant. That was the way it should be. But unfortunately for Michael, with his non-diverse upbringing, he didn't think he would ever escape that panicky voice in the back of his head yelling: "Don't do anything stupid!"

His constant worrying about causing offense only made the whole situation worse. He was already worried about what President Hart was going to ask of him, and now he was worried that he might do or say something stupid on top it. But, thankfully, President Hart was a natural leader. He seemed to sense the discomfort and worry that Michael felt, and he smoothed it out in their initial greetings as he asked about their children, asked about Michael's work, and asked how they were doing in their ward.

See, this is what a leader is like, Michael said to himself. This is how I can never be. Michael was comfortable in his blue dress shirt without a tie. He wasn't made for white shirts and suits. That was the realm of men like President Hart.

"I didn't ask you here to extend any callings," President Hart abruptly said.

And with those words, it felt like a weight had been lifted off of Michael's chest. Kate, too, seemed relieved. President Hart laughed.

"You could have had your secretary tell us that when he made the appointment," Kate said.

"I know. I could have," President Hart said, and he smiled at them, a playful smile.

Michael chuckled. With all the time President Hart sacrifices to serve the stake, I guess I can't begrudge him a little fun, Michael thought.

"So what can we do for you?" Michael asked. "Now that I know it's not a new calling, I'm ready to agree to anything."

"Nothing for me. Nothing even for the church really, not directly at least. I called you here to ask you to do something for the state. Have you heard much about Proposition 8?"

"Sure," Michael said. He had heard about it. Who hadn't? The California Supreme Court had decided that the law was whatever they said it was and had declared same-sex marriages legal. Proposition 8 was the chance for the citizens of California to slap the arrogant judges upside the head and tell them, "No, actually, that's not what the law means." It seemed like a decent enough idea, but it wasn't something that Michael followed with that much interest. California was California. Sure, same-sex marriage didn't make a whole lot of sense, but this was California. Tomorrow they might declare that blue must henceforth be called orange. Would that be a surprise at all?

"The leadership of the church is asking the members here to get involved, both with their time as well as with their wealth. This is a significant decision the state is about to make. We want to persuade California to make the right one."

Michael was skeptical. "Does it really matter in the long run though?" he asked. "Won't some other judges just throw out Proposition 8 like they throw out whatever other laws they don't like?"

"Maybe. You're right, they might do that. But they also might not. Not all judges have forgotten what it means to be part of the judiciary instead of the legislature. But even if they have forgotten and they choose to twist the law to overrule Proposition 8, think of what a victory for Proposition 8 would mean. When the people of California were given the chance to make their voices heard, they declared that marriage should remain what it has always been: the union of a man and a woman."

Kate was fidgeting in her seat. Wait, Michael thought, is she going to cry?

"What's wrong, Sister Keeler?" President Hart asked, following the Mormon custom of addressing members as "Brother" or "Sister" along with their last name.

"I just don't see why ... well ... We don't drink alcohol, but we don't try to ban it either. Yes, homosexual relationships, I understand that they're wrong. But people have free agency, right? Shouldn't they have a choice? So why are we against same-sex marriage?"

President Hart sat back in his chair and clasped his hands together in front of him. "But no one is trying to ban same-sex relationships, Sister Keeler," he said. "Can't you see that that is why your comparison fails? We're not trying to criminalize anything. We're not trying to put people in jail. What we're saying is that marriage should remain the union of a man and a woman. That's all that this is about."

"I just don't see why it matters that much," Kate replied. "Why can't we just let them get same-sex married if that's what they want to do? Because even if same-sex marriage is allowed, that doesn't mean churches will have to change their doctrine and officiate them, that doesn't mean teachers will encourage students to be same-sex married, that doesn't mean people will be forced to help celebrate relationships they view as sinful—bakers aren't going to be forced to bake same-sex wedding cakes, photographers aren't going to be forced to take same-sex wedding pictures.

None of those things are going to happen, so what does it hurt? We know right and wrong, but others disagree. Isn't this just something that we can disagree about?"

President Hart leaned forward. "I understand what you're saying," he told Kate. "I really do. But what I want you to understand is that there is right and wrong, yes, but there is also helpful and harmful. Marriage is the bedrock of our society, Sister Keeler. God has decreed that. Nature has decreed that. And removing such a foundational aspect from marriage as its joint male and female characteristic will have an effect, both on society as well as religion."

"But people are always comparing same-sex marriage to interracial marriage," Kate blurted out. "And aren't they a little right? Isn't opposing same-sex marriage similar to opposing interracial marriage?"

Michael couldn't believe Kate had brought up racism in front of President Hart. My wife is the bravest woman in the world! he said to himself, glancing at President Hart to see if he was upset by her remark.

But rather than act in any way annoyed or offended, President Hart just waved away her comment and settled back in his chair, his hands clasped together in front of him again. "That's just marketing strategy," he told her. "Everyone in our generation knows that opposing interracial marriage was bad, so if same-sex marriage proponents can tie the two together, then they win by default. But ask yourself this: Why did people oppose interracial marriage?"

"Because *they* were racists," Michael said, putting just the right amount of extra stress on "they."

"Right, which meant that they thought what about black people?"

"That they were less than them," Michael answered, proud to be able to answer that question while looking President Hart in the eyes. "Different. Which was wrong of course."

Then President Hart turned back to Kate, who had grown quiet. "Sister Keeler, you know someone who identifies as gay, don't you? Is this what your concern is about?"

Kate blushed a little and looked at the floor, one of her legs folded tightly over the other. "Well, there's a woman in our PTA. She's really nice and she's always so involved."

"Okay. And do you think that she is less than you?"

"No, of course not. She's great."

President Hart paused for a moment. Then he asked, "But should she be having sex with a woman?"

Kate's blush turned bright red. She wasn't accustomed to hearing sex spoken of so bluntly in a church setting. "Well … no," she said.

"Do you see the difference now? Do you see why opposition to interracial marriage and opposition to same-sex marriage are fundamentally different? Think about what you oppose—the behavior. That is where the difference lies. The link only comes from politics and marketing. But you know your own heart. You know why you should oppose same-sex marriage, and you know it has nothing to do with thinking less of anyone. It's the action, not the person. That's what it is. Ignore the marketing and the politics. You know your own heart. Don't let anyone tell you otherwise. Your friend in the PTA is not worth less than you, she's worth just the same. She has her choice in how she will live her life, but you have a choice in whether or not society allows same-sex marriages. You get to look at the benefits, you get to look at the costs. You have a choice, the same as anyone else."

Kate was silent for a moment. Then, still not looking at President Hart, she asked, "Do we have to support Proposition 8?"

"What do you mean?"

"Do we have to support Proposition 8, or does the church give us a choice?"

President Hart's brows tightened. He obviously didn't like the implications of the question. "You always have a choice, Sister Keeler, always. And the church is not going to ask you how you voted. But understand this: The leadership of the church is taking this issue very, very seriously and they want you to take it seriously as well. They are warning you that this is important. I understand what you hear in the media. I understand that you feel for your friends. But do you trust the guidance of the leaders of the church? They are warning you that this is important, Sister Keeler."

Kate didn't respond. Michael felt for her. She believed in the teachings of the church. She believed in its leaders. But she was being asked to take a very unpopular position, and she was so empathetic she couldn't fail to feel pain for those who would be hurt by it. For Michael it wasn't a big deal. He was allergic to people. Why would it matter if they ostracized him? But Kate enjoyed being around others. This was going to be a hard decision for her.

"Perhaps it would help if you explained more about how same-sex marriage is harmful?" Michael said to President Hart, hoping that that would help Kate feel more comfortable with what she was being asked to do. It was a no-brainer for Michael. Same-sex marriage made no sense to him. The only reason marriage had even been invented was to bind a man and a woman together, and the only reason why that mattered, for society anyway, was because society needed men and women to join together and have kids. A society would have to be suicidal to not prefer male-female unions over all other relationships, and what better way to prefer them than to have a specific relationship set up to recognize them, and what better relationship to use than the one that had always been used: marriage. Muck up that word and we'll just have to create another. It all made perfect sense to Michael. So it wasn't a big deal for him—although he was starting to get a little worried about what exactly President Hart was going to ask them to do—but he hoped that Kate could see the logic behind it as well. She rarely listened to Michael about politics, but perhaps she would listen to their stake president.

President Hart sighed. Michael wondered how many of these conversations he was having and how often he had to justify the church's opposition to same-sex marriage to members who should already understand it.

"Okay, let's look at it from the point of view of society," President Hart said. "We need marriage. It's critical to the survival of our nation. Because of this, it's in our best interest to hold it up as the ideal and to keep it separate from all other relationships in terms of importance. We cannot create a co-equal relationship to marriage and then expect it to not diminish the importance and centrality of marriage in our society, and we cannot diminish the importance and centrality of marriage in our society without seriously harming society itself."

Michael watched Kate's reaction. She was listening to President Hart. Why doesn't she ever listen to me about things like this? Michael wondered.

"Also, we worry so much about the government debts we are leaving behind for our children and our grandchildren," President Hart said. "Shouldn't we worry more about the impact our actions will have on them morally? The idea that holding up same-sex marriage as equally important to marriage will not affect the sexuality of some in the rising generation is pure blindness if not outright deceit. Why would we want to introduce a change that is sure to create problems in the lives of others? We don't have to support same-sex marriage. We have a choice. Why would we want to support it, knowing that negative implications must come? We are not immutable rocks, forged from birth for a single path alone. If society starts holding up an alternate path and preaching that it is just as valid, some are going to be influenced to take that path who would not have done so without society's encouragement and guidance. But I know this is an uncomfortable truth for many to consider, so we don't need to discuss this particular reason any further. I think I've said enough about it."

Michael, for one, was a little caught off guard by this train of thought. But Kate didn't seem the least bit surprised by it.

"Those are some of the reasons why it is harmful to society," President Hart continued, "but it is also harmful to society because it is harmful to religion, and religion is the core of society. Why is good good? What values should we hold? What manner of men and women should we be? These are questions that can only be answered through religious beliefs of some sort, and it is only formal religion which provides a parent with the means of successfully passing along their values to their children, to their grandchildren, and on and on.

"To understand why same-sex marriage is harmful to religion, consider what a society is saying when it legalizes it. First, consider this: Are same-sex marriages necessary? Imagine a world where same-sex attraction didn't exist. Would same-sex marriage exist in that world? No, of course not—because same-sex marriage isn't needed. It wasn't needed in the past. It isn't needed in the present. It won't be needed in the future. The only reason why same-sex marriage is even a consideration is because some people *want* to be same-sex married. Now, someone playing devil's advocate might ask: But what if normal attraction didn't exist, wouldn't marriage itself not be necessary in that world? To which I would answer: If normal attraction didn't exist, then humans wouldn't exist either. That's the point. Normal attraction is needed, therefore marriage is needed. Same-sex marriage, however, is not."

Kate was shuffling uncomfortably in her seat. Michael hoped she didn't think that President Hart was saying that the people themselves were unneeded. It was a tricky point to make.

"Why, then, would a society choose to legalize same-sex marriage?" President Hart asked. "Some people want to be same-sex married, yes, but some people want lots of things and that doesn't mean that we bend society to allow them. Why then would we legalize same-sex marriage? Here is the answer: We wouldn't. We might, however, legalize gay marriage. And it is in the difference between same-sex marriage and gay marriage that the harm to religion can be found."

"I don't understand what you're saying," Kate said, a confused look on her face. "I thought same-sex marriage and gay marriage were the same thing."

"Here is the question for you, Sister Keeler," President Hart said. "Before California's Supreme Court imposed their will over the law, was gay marriage legal?"

"Well, no; I thought that was the point of Proposition 8? To erase the ruling of the activist judges?"

"Actually, I'm not sure that you are right. Consider this: What does it mean to be gay? If being gay just means feeling same-sex attraction, then gay marriage has always been legal. When have we ever cared if a man feels same-sex attraction yet still chooses to marry a woman? Why in the world would that matter so long as his wife is not deceived and the man is committed to living faithfully to her? Why in the world would we care what attractions he has chosen to ignore?"

And how would we ever know? Michael thought. It's not like people rush around disclosing their deepest struggles. And what if it isn't even a deep struggle? What if it's no more than a minor annoyance that's simple for them to set aside? We'd never know.

"And what if being gay means that you engage in same-sex intimacy?" President Hart asked. "Again, do we block people from marrying who have made past mistakes in their lives? Of course not. And the sad fact is that some will choose to violate their commitment and continue acting in that way despite their marriage."

"But that's not what people mean when they talk about gay marriage," Kate said.

"Exactly. And that's what is so harmful to religion. They're not talking about attraction. They're not talking about action. They're talking about both. Think about that. They're saying that to be gay is both attraction *and* action. They're combining the two together, making it seem like there is no separation at all. Can't you see how dangerous it is when people refuse to acknowledge the separation? Religions preach against behavior, but now society is claiming that some types of behavior are actually classes of *being*, cutting the behavior off from any expectation that it can and should be resisted. Can't you see what is happening? How can religion preach against sin when some people *are* sin? How can you preach against lying when lying is what some people *are*? How can you preach against stealing when stealing is what some people *are*? How can you preach against adultery when adultery is what some people *are*?"

Kate's eyes opened a bit at this explanation. Michael felt a little jealous. Why couldn't he be as persuasive?

"We've walked into a trap, Sister Keeler. And we can't escape the trap because any attempt at reason is always met with 'racism this' or 'racism that.' You proved that yourself by your comparison of same-sex marriage and interracial marriage. We're paralyzed by guilt for society's past wrongs, so we cast off the very idea of sin lest it stain our hands with the accusation of bigotry. We're trapped. We can't preach against sin because people now *are* sin, so to preach against sin is to preach against people and to preach against people is just like what the racists did, and we don't want to be horrible bigots like the racists, do we? Can't you see, Sister Keeler? It's a trap. It's a cunning, well-laid trap."

President Hart paused and looked up at the wall behind him. Michael turned to see what he was looking at. There were two pictures there. One was of the Savior, arms outstretched, standing amidst the clouds. The other was of the current First Presidency, the three men who led the Mormon church. Michael wasn't sure which picture President Hart was looking at—perhaps both, perhaps neither.

Then President Hart continued. "Society might have lost all interest in God and in seeking His help against the wiles of the adversary, but that doesn't mean that the adversary has lost any interest in us. He's constantly weaving strong cords to bind us, and he can wait as long as he has to. He's a devious bastard."

Michael leaned forward in his chair, surprised by that final word. Did President Hart just say bastard? Hey, if he can say bastard, then I can say bastard! Michael looked sideways at his wife to catch her reaction. She was still looking at President Hart, but somehow she read Michael's mind. She kicked his foot discretely.

Okay, fine, Michael thought, I guess I won't say it in front of Kate. He thought what President Hart had said was great. Sure, it's not the way he would have described it. He would have just said, "Listen, Kate, all this support for same-sex marriage is just crazy talk!" But that's why President Hart was a stake president and Michael would never be. And Kate seemed to have been affected by his words. She was more calm now. Still upset, and Michael worried she still might cry, but there was a firmness to her now. She had been convinced to make a decision, and now she was going to stick with it no matter the cost.

"And that is why we are asking you to support Proposition 8," President Hart continued. "Same-sex marriage is unnecessary and the argument for gay marriage is inherently dehumanizing. If people are sin, then people are not people. They're just blobs of flesh following biological impulses, no initiative, no personal choice—no humanity at all. When judges declare there is no rational basis for marriage, they are declaring there is no rational reason to view a human as a human. When they declare that same-sex marriage must be allowed due to equal protection, they are declaring that we are not men and women with the agency to chart our own lives; instead we're just a blurred combination of attraction and action, no self-determination, nothing more than preprogrammed robots. Is it any wonder that the religious, with our optimistic view of God's children, reject such a debasing argument? We know better than that. You said it yourself, Sister Keeler: we have free agency. All of us do. We are not sin. We are not attraction. We are humans, men and women, sons and daughters of God."

He paused and looked at the two of them.

"How can we help?" Kate asked, all doubt and worry vanished from her face.

President Hart smiled and nodded at her. I've got to learn how to do that, Michael said to himself. Maybe it's the suit.

"The campaign will be an expensive one," President Hart told them. "We're asking those that can afford it to strongly consider donating in favor of Proposition 8."

Money? Michael thought. I can do money. He had been worried that he would be asked to go door to door or something. For a man allergic to people, such a request would be like asking him to walk into the flames of Hell and to take a swim in a burning magma pool.

"Do you have a specific amount you expect from us?" Kate asked.

President Hart shook his head. "I'm going to leave that up to you. I just ask that you remember that this is one of the most significant campaigns you will have the opportunity to take part in. Please support it. Please be generous."

And that was that. Kate was on board and Michael had never been off board. Driving home after the meeting, Michael considered President Hart's explanation of the difference between same-sex marriage and gay marriage, and the more he thought about it, the more distinct the terms became in his mind. Same-sex marriage, while pointless and harmful, seemed as if its impact could be contained enough for the wise to work around. Gay marriage, on the other hand—with its baggage of *being* and the trap that creates—seemed catastrophic.

Kate was thinking through the discussion as well. She kept repeating how much she admired President Hart and how clear he made such a murky situation.

"Do you know anything about his kids?" she asked. "Does he have a son? He'd have to be a bit older of course. At least nine, nine to twelve. He'd have to be taller too, but President Hart is tall so I'm sure his sons would be—"

Michael almost swerved into oncoming traffic, "Grizzy is only eight years old!"

Kate gave Michael a soft punch in the arm and said, "Calm down. What does it hurt to think about who she might marry?"

"She's only eight years old! I don't want to imagine that! Ask me when she's thirty or something."

"Do you honestly want your daughter to be unmarried at thirty?"

"Fine, fine, but wait until she's twenty at least. She's eight. Eight!"

Kate dropped the subject, but she hummed to herself the rest of the way home, songs that to Michael all sounded vaguely like the soundtrack to a wedding reception.

Later that night, they sat together in front of their computer, trying to decide how much to donate to the cause. Michael thought they should sleep on it, but Kate insisted on doing it that night. Michael wondered if maybe she was worried she might lose her nerve if they waited until morning.

"I'm thinking $100," Michael said, feeling immensely generous until Kate turned around and gave him one of her looks—not one of her good looks, one of her other looks.

"Michael," she said, "we're spending $5,000 on our cruise next month and you expect us to spend only $100 on this? Marriage is the foundation of society, Michael. I'm not going to have California mess it up just because we were too stingy to help when we could."

It was their ten-year anniversary, and they were splurging beyond splurging for the cruise. Why couldn't Proposition 8 have happened on one of our normal years where our vacation is camping with the kids? Michael said to himself, worried about what amount Kate might decide was appropriate.

"I think we should give at least ten percent of what we spend on the cruise," Kate said.

"Ten percent? But that's $500!"

"Right, $500 for each of us, making $1,000." Kate typed in the amount and hit enter.

NO! Michael screamed inside, seeing the vision of his new golf clubs melting away. But Kate had already input the credit card info and submitted the donation.

President Hart, what have you done to me, President Hart? But, deprived of his golf clubs or not, Michael was proud of Kate for what she was doing. The money was hard for him, but money can always be re-earned and he had a feeling that this was going to end up costing Kate more than him in the end.

The weeks passed and before Michael knew it, they were on their cruise. With the large crowds on the cruise ship, Michael reached his limit for human contact quickly, but it was all worth it to sit on the balcony of their room, his arm around Kate, and stare at the deep blue of the open ocean with her, the waves rising and falling as far as the eye could see. The worries of the office and of politics were gone. He did worry a bit about Grizzy—Michael was the one who passed the worrying gene on to her in the first place—but he was happy to find her no worse upon their return than she had been before, or so he thought at first.

Then she stopped sleeping.

It started innocently enough. They had watched a movie and she had gotten scared by it. Lots of kids go through that. But Grizzy wouldn't let go. Not every night, thankfully, but too often. It was like some sort of crazy cycle. She'd start getting scared at night and wouldn't sleep without a lot of attention from Michael and Kate, and then she'd be fine for a few nights, making them think it was all over, but then it'd start up again.

Sometimes Kate brought Grizzy into bed to sleep with them, but Michael was always uncomfortable with that. Parent's beds weren't meant for kids to sleep in. Parent's beds were meant for parents to sleep in and, on good nights, for parents to make new kids in. He was also a bit harsher than Kate, willing to let Grizzy cry herself to sleep alone in her room while Kate would rather hug her and comfort her and take her down on the couch to sleep together. We're such softies in the twenty-first century! Michael told himself, imagining cave men sending their fearful daughters out of the cave to sleep in the dark with the saber-toothed tigers and woolly mammoths.

Then Grizzy's hands started to crack.

They knew she was washing them more than she need to. But, hey, who likes germs anyway? Still, this was too much. Cracked hands was something that Michael had to deal with, not something that his eight-year old daughter should be going through. They looked online for help. They bought a couple books and started going through them. They even considered a therapist, maybe medication. But come on, Grizzy was just eight years old! That just seemed too drastic of a step.

One quiet evening, Kate was working through one of the worry exercises with Grizzy in the family room, Michael resting on his recliner and trying to forget the horrible breath his last patient had had. Then they both realized that the house was too quiet.

"Where's Mikey?" Kate asked, referring to Tank.

If you want to name the kids, then you can birth them yourself! she had told Michael when he had said he wanted to name their daughter Grizelda in honor of a rescued princess from a forgotten video game he had played in his youth. So Grizzy's name was Aspen and Tank's name was Michael, but Michael figured that his participation in the whole birthing process deserved at least a token benefit, so he assigned them their nicknames. To Kate they were Aspen and Mikey, but to Michael they would forever be Grizzy and Tank.

"I don't know," Michael answered, trying to come up with some clever reply before realizing that a silent three-year old Tank was probably a bad thing, potentially a *very* bad thing.

He sprang up out of the chair and hurried to the front room, then the kitchen. No Tank.

"Panther, do you know where Tank is?" Michael asked their German shepherd, who was sleeping on the floor, her legs kicking as she dreamed of younger days. Panther had been Michael's dog before he had married Kate, hence he got to name her. Old and ornery, she avoided the overly rambunctious Tank like the plague. If Panther was in the kitchen, then Tank was somewhere far away.

"Check the storage room," Kate called to Michael.

"You mean the panic room?" Michael said.

"The storage room!"

It was a good suggestion. Tank always loved playing among the food storage containers in the panic room. Kate might call it a storage room, but it actually truly was a panic room. Michael didn't know the story, but apparently one of the previous owners of their house had been somewhat paranoid, hence the panic room: a small room upstairs with no windows, with metal-reinforced walls and door and a steel crossbar that could be dropped into place, locking the world safely outside.

Tank loved to play in the panic room. Probably something to do with his XY chromosomes since Grizzy didn't particularly like it much. Tank could often be found there, building forts among the food storage cans. Mormons are known for their food storage, and Michael and Kate had accumulated plenty. In decades past, Mormons stored multiple years' worth of food. That was in the days of the Cold War and the, at times very plausible, threat of a nuclear winter. Today, Mormon food storage was meant for more short-term threats like natural disasters, terrorist strikes, or layoffs, which meant that only a few months of food were needed instead of multiple years. But beyond the banal worrying of tornadoes, hurricanes, or short-sighted executives, Michael was mindful of a more pressing problem: zombies.

"We don't need a panic room," Kate had told Michael when they had first moved into the house.

"But what about when the zombies attack? When that first zombie breaks through the door, you're going to be happy you have a panic room to hide in."

"Zombies aren't real, Michael," Kate said, an annoyed tone to her voice.

"Yet. They aren't real—yet. But when they are, boy, is that panic room going to come in handy!"

"It's not a panic room. It's a storage room."

"It's a panic room."

"Storage room."

"But the zombies …"

"Storage room!"

The argument brought two thoughts to Michael's mind. First, how in the world had he convinced Kate to marry him? Second, what good is a food cache in the midst of a zombie apocalypse if he didn't have some means of protection as well? The answer was obvious: he needed a gun cache, too.

"We are not getting any guns," Kate had told him.

"What? Do you expect me to fight off the zombies with my old golf clubs?"

"We are *not* getting any guns!"

"And when they come to eat our brains and make us as brainless as they are?"

Then Kate got quiet, her annoyed expression replaced

by her clever one. Michael hated that expression. It meant the argument was already over.

"Fine," Kate said, smiling prettily at him. "You can buy a gun, but first you have to take a gun safety course."

And that was the end of it. Kate was no fool. Sure, Michael had to put up with people at church because church was church and church was important, and he had to put up with people at work because that paid the bills, but there was no way that Michael was going to choose to sit in a classroom full of people—honestly, how he managed to deal with his patients was anyone's guess (perhaps their inability to talk during their dental checkups helped him cope)—so there was no way he was going to sit through a gun safety course. She had won without even having to tell him no. So, no guns, and his old golf clubs got stored in the panic room along with the food storage. Kate thought he had put them there because he never had time to play golf anyway, but Michael had another use in mind. He would have stored his new golf clubs there too, had things worked out differently, but they had not and it was just as well. He had no time for golf anyway, and an old club was just as good at bashing in zombie skulls as a new one.

"Tank, are you in there?" Michael called after he came up the stairs and turned the corner toward the panic room. "You know Mom doesn't like you playing in there."

He heard a giggle and the sound of moving cans. Yup, Tank was in there all right.

"What are you doing—" Michael asked, rounding the doorway and finding Tank standing on the top of a pile of condensed milk cans.

"Superman!" Tank called, swinging his arms and jumping off the cans.

"Tank!" Michael yelled, rushing forward and catching the boy, whose weight drove them both onto the floor. "What are you doing? You'll break an arm doing that!"

"I was playing Superman," Tank said. "Like yesterday."

Yesterday? And then Michael remembered. They had stacked the couch pillows up and Michael had had Tank jump off the couch onto them. Kate had been annoyed, but Tank had laughed. What am I teaching my kids? Michael asked himself. I'm such a horrible father.

Of course, Tank's arms were so thick the padding would probably prevent any damage. Tank was thick everywhere. Michael sometimes wondered if the thickness extended to the inside of Tank's head, leaving very little space for a brain. He didn't share this thought with Kate of course. Doing that would certainly cause her to switch into roommate mode, and Michael hated when Kate was in roommate mode.

But Tank didn't break his arm that summer. And, although Grizzy didn't get any better, at least she didn't get any worse. The nation, however, went absolutely insane. The presidential election was like nothing Michael could remember. The craziness extended even into his own office. Rick especially was caught up in it, constantly talking about the election, about some speech, some saying. Eventually, Michael had to ban all talk of politics in his office in order to preserve his sanity.

After one particularly long day, Michael came home and flopped onto his recliner. Rick had been so enthused about the latest speech that he couldn't stop talking about it, ban or no ban, and it seemed like every patient who sat down in the dental chair had not brushed for weeks. Now, sitting there in his recliner, Michael could still hear the blathering bouncing around in his ears and he could still smell the stench swirling around in his nostrils. He needed to distract himself somehow but didn't have the energy to do anything productive. I'll just watch TV, he decided. But he'd have to wait a bit before anything worthwhile came on. The sci-fi movies didn't start until later. Right now it would only be lame reality shows.

Panther rubbed her nose on his leg until he started petting her head.

You're getting old, girl, Michael thought, sad to see all the gray on her face. How is it that your breath smells better than my patients'? Should I tell them to start eating dog food? Is that the secret?

Why in the world did I choose to become a dentist? Michael asked himself, as he often did. But it paid great, and the schedule wasn't bad, so who was he to complain about it?

Of course, the schedule would be better if I could work from home, Michael thought. Hey, this is the twenty-first century! Shouldn't someone have invented remote-controlled robots for this by now? I could sit in my recliner here at home and remotely clean people's teeth via robot. Why isn't that possible? Why hasn't someone invented that yet?

Kate was reading a book to Tank, who didn't seem to be listening very well. Grizzy was in the kitchen doing her homework.

"Kate, I think Grizzy should be a robotics engineer," Michael told her.

Kate looked up from her book. "She's only eight. And why not Mikey? He likes robots."

Tank in fact was playing with a robot right then, a plastic action figure, which he repeatedly bashed into the carpet, his thick arm raising and lowering the toy again and again and again, his thick, thick arm. Michael looked at Tank's head.

"Kate, I think Grizzy should be a robotics engineer," Michael repeated.

From time to time over the weeks that passed, church members were asked to rally in favor of Proposition 8, but Michael always found some excuse to keep his family away. He supported the initiative of course, but the thought of standing on some street corner and waving a sign nearly gave him a panic attack. He figured he was doing the movement a favor by staying away. They didn't want their crowd of smiling faces spoiled by his sour expression.

Then Election Day finally came, and the Democrats got their historic moment and California got its Proposition 8. Kate refused to tell Michael which presidential candidate she had voted for, which meant her vote had probably canceled his own, but she did tell him she had voted for Proposition 8, and he had too, and they had given some money to help it along, and it had won, and now it was over.

Except it wasn't.

The backlash started as soon as everyone realized that Proposition 8 had won. Anger was the word of the day. Activists marched in the street, yelling at people, yelling at churches, yelling at whoever or whatever they could blame for not getting their way.

Like most, Michael kept his head down. The anger was unpleasant, and it was easiest to just avoid it. But that often proved impossible, and two words started popping up in the media whenever people spoke about same-sex marriage: "marriage equality." What a misleading pile of marketing fluff, Michael thought the first time he heard it. Not that its inaccuracy was out of place compared to other political slogans—"pro-choice" is not in favor of all choices, "pro-life" is not in favor of all life—but the insincerity of the words still bothered him. Same-sex marriage activists were marching underneath a banner of "marriage equality" when equality wasn't what they were actually seeking—they were seeking same-sex marriage, not equality, just same-sex marriage. It made Michael wish he could halt their speeches, look them in the eye, and ask: "If person A wants to marry person B, will you always say yes?"

The honest answer, of course, would be "No." The activists weren't idiots. They knew that for marriage to mean anything, it needed guidelines. The only difference was with same-sex marriage: they wanted to allow it, but Michael didn't. So the conflict was about same-sex marriage, not about "marriage equality," and the insincerity and outright bias of the media was beginning to drive Michael nuts.

Kate was having an even harder time than Michael. She felt for those that sought a same-sex marriage. She longed for a resolution. And she was thankful for the privacy of the voting booth, thankful that as the rage flew all around her, she was able to stay quiet and safe.

But safety was short-lived. This wasn't a simple political disagreement, like an argument about taxes, where both sides thought the other side was wrong but both sides still allowed the other side to remain human. The advocates for same-sex marriage were demonizing their opponents. Any that opposed same-sex marriage didn't simply oppose it; they were anti-gay, they were homophobes, they were bigots, they were haters who wanted to take the rights of loving citizens away. And it wasn't right for such horrible bigots to sleep peacefully in their beds or to work successfully in their careers. It wasn't right that any of those horrible bigots should walk free after they had committed the unpardonable sin of standing against "marriage equality."

And there were too many that still opposed same-sex marriage. All of them needed to learn that that opinion would not be tolerated. Examples needed to be made. And so the list of all the donors of Proposition 8 was released, and the names were shared far and wide, anonymous websites gleefully posting the personal details of the potential targets, newspapers helpfully making the list easy for activists to search.

The impact reached Michael the very next day. Coming into his office that morning, he was surprised to see the front desk vacant.

"Where's Rick?" he asked the rest of his staff.

All of them seemed to look in different directions.

"Where's Rick? Is he sick today?"

"Rick quit," someone finally replied.

"What do you mean he quit? No two weeks' notice? Not even a good-bye?"

More silence. Then finally someone told Michael, "Didn't you know that Rick is gay?"

"What?" Michael said. "Uh ... no, I didn't." He never paid attention to the personal lives of his staff. Not the best quality in a boss, but at least he wasn't nosy.

"He's been living with his boyfriend for two years. They were hoping to be same-sex married."

I thought he lived with his mother, Michael said to himself, surprised at how little he actually knew his staff.

It wasn't just Michael, either. A man who worked at a theater was forced to resign; a restaurant was being picketed. Other examples were being made as well. "What did they expect?" voices replied. "They paid to steal the rights away from others!"

The next strike was against Kate, who came home from a PTA meeting one night, her cheeks wet with tears.

"What's wrong?" Michael asked as he shut the dishwasher and turned it on.

Kate set her purse down. "Well, at least I'll have more free nights," she managed to say before bursting into tears and burying her face in her hands as she sank into a seat at the table.

Michael considered asking what she meant, but he thought he already knew: Proposition 8 donors were apparently not welcome in the PTA anymore.

The next strike was a message on Michael's dental office door. He arrived one morning to find the word "BIGOT!" written in black marker. At least they didn't throw a rock through my window, he thought as he taped a magazine page over the slur on the door. The page showed a picture of a sunny beach, a happy couple lounging on their towels as they looked out at the sunset. Michael's anniversary cruise seemed like so long ago.

Then the phone calls started. Michael had hired a sweet old lady named Gretchen to manage the front desk, but she couldn't handle the abuse. Michael reported the harassment to the police, but the officer taking his report didn't appear very interested.

"You've got to understand," the officer told him. "When you donate to such an emotionally charged issue, you're going to end up the target of angry activists."

Michael was shocked by the response. "So basically the bullies win?" he said.

"Sorry, man, but it is what it is. I don't make the rules," the officer replied.

The response disheartened Michael. It seemed as if the officer was telling him it was all his fault. Michael understood common sense. He understood that it needed to be used in order to avoid trouble because life wasn't perfect and it was best to avoid trouble if you could. You don't walk down dark alleys alone at night, not if you don't want to be robbed. Michael understood that. But was that what society had become? Was participating in the political process now as dangerous as walking down a dark alley? How had we fallen so far?

And the calls didn't stop, so Gretchen eventually had to quit. She offered two weeks' notice but Michael didn't take it. He could see how the abuse was wearing on her. She hadn't asked for this, and it would be easier for her to work somewhere else, to work for someone who wasn't being targeted. And that was the point, wasn't it? Everyone needed to see how much pain they would feel if they supported the wrong side of this issue. Everyone needed to learn their lesson.

For Gretchen's replacement, Michael hired an ex-marine named John, who had dodged bullets in Afghanistan and Iraq and was unfazed by the threat of mean phone calls. But John was no Rick. Rick had had a presence about him, a positivity—almost a hyperness—that filled the office whenever he was there, cheering up the rest of the staff. Michael missed Rick and the fun conversations they used to have. Rick had had an honest interest in Michael and in Michael's life. It made Michael feel guilty now to know he had never bothered to learn anything about Rick in return.

"So, John," he said one afternoon as the day was wrapping up. "You aren't married, are you?"

"No," John said, looking up from a magazine he was reading.

"Any significant other?"

"No."

"Dating anyone?"

"No."

Michael looked at John, who stared back blankly.

"Anything interesting I should know about you?" Michael asked.

"No."

"Alright then."

Michael retreated to his office and sat down in front of his computer. The website bookmark was still there for the golf clubs he had wanted to buy what seemed like a life-time ago. They didn't even appeal to him now. He clicked through articles on a few websites, wasting the time before he would head for home, when he came across a political ad for same-sex marriage. Some sort of actress—Michael couldn't remember her name—dressed simply but fashionably with a piece of duct tape covering her mouth and a slogan on her cheek. Michael had seen the ad before but it had been a different celebrity that time. He wondered if this actress cared more about the cause or about being known as a supporter of the cause. With the pretty and the popular, you never really could be sure. And what was written on her cheek? Was it an attempt to justify same-sex marriage? Was it a positive message explaining why same-sex marriage was necessary and good? No. The message was "No Hate."

Hate. Opposition to same-sex marriage was being smeared as nothing more than hate. Marketing relies on emotional manipulation, and this was marketing, plain and simple, with a premise as basic as high school itself: Do you want to hang with the cool kids or do you want to be a hateful bigot? Get in line. Conform. Dissent will not be tolerated.

Michael found it strange. Why can't they justify their opinion without attacking those who disagree? What is it about the same-sex marriage movement that drives them to paint their opponents as bigots? Is that really the only argument they have?

But just as the harassing calls at his office had become less of a problem, they started coming to his home as well.

Michael turned off the ringer and started to screen their calls, but then one night a white-faced Grizzy walked into the family room to tell Michael, "Someone said a bad word on the answering machine." Michael disconnected it that night.

Grizzy was getting worse. Michael and Kate had done what they could to keep the abuses hidden from her, but she was sensitive and could sense the tension that Michael and Kate were living under. She was eating less and less, worried she might vomit, worried about poison, worried about anything and everything.

Michael and Kate began talking seriously about getting her therapy, but they hesitated, worried that whatever therapist they picked would view them not as her loving parents but as hateful bigots. Would the therapist try to turn their daughter against them? Would the therapist see it as a duty to "reeducate" their daughter rather than to simply help her with her worries? Maybe it was an irrational fear, but it was an irrational time. And if people really believed that Michael and Kate were as horrible as their slurs made it sound, why wouldn't it happen?

Then somehow Michael's cell phone number got leaked onto the Internet. In a way, he was glad it had happened. If his family faced abuse, he'd rather it was directed at him instead of his wife and kids. He wondered, though, as he listened to the angry callers. Do these people know anything about me other than that I donated to Proposition 8? Was that the only instruction they were given before being set loose to take out their anger on a stranger? And anger was all it was.

"You bigot, what harm is it to you if someone else gets married? You're just a bigot."

"You evil Nazi!"

"How'd you like it if someone took away your rights, you homophobe!"

"What you did was evil!"

"We don't tolerate bigotry!"

One night Michael lay awake in bed. Kate was downstairs sleeping on the couch with Grizzy, who was on a third night of not sleeping alone. Michael looked up at the ceiling, remembering the last call he had gotten on his cell phone. It had come as he was leaving his office. The words were as unkind as they usually were. It made him wonder again: Why does the same-sex marriage movement treat all who disagree as if they were bigots? Why can't they let me remain a person, an actual person who simply doesn't agree with them? He couldn't understand it, and as he lay awake and wished for sleep, he debated with them in his mind, imagining what they would say to him.

"Everyone must support same-sex marriage! If you don't, you're a bigot!"

"Hey, let's be reasonable here—"

"Because racism!"

"Wait, what? Where'd the preposition go? And what does that have to do with anything anyway? That's not what we're talking about—"

"Because racism!"

"Do all your arguments depend on past guilt? Can't you talk about this without smearing others as bigots?"

"Because racism!"

"No, seriously. You keep saying that, and I'm thinking about what you're saying, and I'm telling you that what you're saying makes no sense. Do you expect me to just shut off my brain and not think? Is that what you're asking for? Is that what you're trying to bully me into doing?"

"Because racism!"

"But—"

"Shut up, bigot! Shut up! Shut up! Shut up!"

He thought again of the political slogan "marriage equality," and suddenly the words took on a more sinister purpose. By framing the discussion in that way, same-sex marriage advocates were claiming that Michael wasn't just opposing same-sex marriage; he was opposing equality itself. And who opposes equality? Bigots do. And what do we do to bigots? We shun them and we spit on them and we kick them out of civil society. Why did they pick this approach? Michael wondered. Why can't they let us remain people who simply disagree? Then, drifting off to sleep, he had one final question for the same-sex marriage advocates: "If same-sex marriage can only come through smearing hundreds of millions as bigots, is it worth the price?"

The phone calls didn't stop. Michael did his best to ignore them, reminding himself that the callers weren't really insulting him, they were just insulting the imaginary monster they thought he was. Thinking of it that way helped a little, but it still stung to be on the receiving end of such anger. And then there were the more threatening calls.

"I hope someone takes away your family too."

Comments like that made Michael worry. People were letting themselves get carried away in anger. Do they even think of us as human anymore? he wondered. Will they rein in their anger at some point, or has it become uncontrollable? And more worrying than the messages was Michael's realization that he could recognize a familiar voice among the callers—the same man was calling again and again. They had a stalker.

Michael tried to talk to him. "Why are you doing this?" But the man only hung up. Then the man called back the next day to make another comment about how hateful and horrible Michael and his family were. This time Michael tried to reach him with a friendly tone. "My favorite ice cream is Neapolitan. What's yours?" But the man only hung up again.

Michael considered calling the police. To have one person focus on him seemed more dangerous than getting calls from random people, but the reaction the police had given to his workplace harassment made him doubt that calling them would do any good. Society had marked Michael and his family as outcasts. They were on their own.

Unable to turn to others for help, Michael decided to take his family's safety into his own hands. He didn't bother taking a gun safety course. He didn't talk to Kate. He just drove to a gun store after work one day and bought a revolver. There was a waiting period before he could claim it, so he couldn't take it home that night. Having to wait made him nervous. People were making themselves angrier and angrier. If nothing stopped the escalation, it was only a matter of time before someone snapped and decided to make things really ugly.

The worsening conditions weren't limited to just Michael and weren't invisible to others. Even some same-sex marriage advocates were starting to call for restraint and to speak out against the witch hunts being held for the Proposition 8 donors. But Michael found the advocates' words to be hollow because right after calling for civility, they would characterize those who disagreed with same-sex marriage as anti-gay, or homophobes, or bigots, or else the advocates would claim there was no rational basis for marriage. They're disingenuous, Michael thought. They can't complain about our treatment in one breath and then demonize us in the next. They are helping to whip the hounds into a frenzy, and then they act shocked when the hounds begin to bite. They're contributing to this hostile environment with the arguments they use to advance their cause. What did they think would happen after they labeled us as bigots? How did they expect others to treat us?

And then Michael realized: That's the point, isn't it? They don't *have* any other arguments. Reality has dealt the same-sex marriage advocates a weak hand. There is no need for same-sex marriage. It wasn't needed in the past. It isn't needed in the present. It won't be needed in the future. Compare that to the utter chaos and collapse that would occur should marriage itself be discarded. Yes, reality has dealt the same-sex marriage advocates a weak hand. They can't argue with logic because the truth is that same-sex marriage isn't necessary, and the religious can sense how harmful gay marriage would be. People are not sin—the very idea is toxic to morality. So what other argument does that leave the same-sex marriage advocates? Michael asked himself. What other method is available to them other than to demonize people like me?

There isn't one, he told himself. We have to be thought of as bigots and homophobes, as hateful people that want to steal away the rights from others. We have to be thought of as bigots because same-sex marriage will never win if people like me are allowed to be seen as reasonable. That's why the advocates are arguing that there is no rational basis for opposing same-sex marriage. That's why they claim that all opposition is nothing but bigotry itself. They're arguing that way because they have to. They're arguing that way because there's no other way for them to win.

But behavior is not being, Michael said to himself. If society realizes that truth, then the whole jig is up. Behavior is not being!

"Shut up, bigot! Shut up! Shut up! Shut up!"

And so, branded as a bigot because he had to be, Michael went to the gun store once the waiting period was over and picked up his revolver. The choice of gun had been the clerk's suggestion. He had immediately sized Michael up as someone unused to guns, and to be honest, the operation of a semi-automatic intimidated Michael, making the revolver seem simple in comparison. Michael had stood in the aisle of the gun store and held the gun up, pointing it at the distant wall. Dry firing a few times to get the feel of it, he imagined himself using the gun to protect his family. The trigger took more pressure to fire than he expected. He hoped he would never have to use it.

After returning home with his revolver in its case and a box full of ammunition, Michael hid the case in his sock drawer. Should I store it loaded? he wondered. That seemed like the wise thing to do if he needed it for self-defense. What good is an unloaded gun when someone is breaking into your home? But the idea of Grizzy finding his gun—or worse, Tank—and accidentally shooting themselves or someone else terrified him, so he left the gun unloaded, the bullets in their box on the other side of the sock drawer. It was dangerous to leave the revolver outside of a gun safe, but Michael felt his family was in a dangerous situation, and he didn't dare make it any harder for him to find his gun.

I just hope I never have to use it, Michael said to himself.

Grizzy continued to have a hard time sleeping. It seemed like every other night Kate was sleeping with her downstairs on the couch. Michael tried to talk with Grizzy, to help her see that her fears were irrational. But she was only eight, and it seemed like her emotions were simply too much for her young mind to control. It was like she were two different people. While talking with him, she could come up with alternate possibilities. No, the food isn't poisonous because my parents would never poison me. Dad, and Mom, and Mikey didn't get poisoned from eating the food, so neither would I. No, the food wasn't poisoned the last time I tried to eat it. She had these rational thoughts. She could identify them. Yet, when she was caught up in the midst of her worries, it didn't seem to do much good. She needed some sort of a boost. Michael and Kate began thinking more seriously about medication and therapy. But who could they trust? With the hostile environment that had been created by the same-sex marriage advocates, an environment that treated people like Michael and Kate as bigots, who could they trust with the well-being of their daughter?

They had Grizzy start brushing Panther's fur every night. It was Kate's idea. She hoped the task would help soothe Grizzy, that the act of serving another would help her forget her worries. Panther loved the attention. She would sit up tall despite her old, trembling legs, patiently letting Grizzy work the brush through her hair. Kate thought that maybe the two would bond, that somehow an animal could help Grizzy in ways that she and Michael could not. And it seemed to help for a while. Grizzy actually slept in her own room for four nights straight. Panther had started sleeping on the floor beside her bed, which Michael thought was helping. But on the fifth night, Grizzy was back looking for Kate again.

"What if Panther dies in the middle of the night?" she asked, tears in her eyes. "What if I wake up and her body is just lying there on my floor?"

And so, down onto the couch Kate and Grizzy went, Panther following behind, the old dog completely unaware that she was only adding to Grizzy's worries rather than removing them.

The phone calls continued, the familiar voice calling again and again to speak hateful remarks. Michael's attempts at reaching the man at a human level didn't work. It was obvious the man had no interest in Michael as a person. To him, Michael was only a bigot, and any evidence to the contrary only seemed to aggravate him; so Michael learned to simply hang up. He wished he could ignore the calls entirely, but the number was always blocked and Michael couldn't ignore blocked calls without risking losing a call from a patient.

It seemed bizarre to devote so much time and energy to harassing a stranger. What would lead someone to act like that? Michael wondered. He didn't know. But he imagined what the stalker must look like. Carrying that much anger inside must mark the man somehow. But how?

At least work didn't get any worse. No one else from his staff quit. He did lose a handful of clients, but he wasn't sure of the reason—there was always some amount of turnover with the number of clients he had: people move, people forget, people stop caring about their teeth. Some clients actually mentioned support for Michael and what he had done. They whispered that they had voted for Proposition 8 and were happy it had passed. But otherwise, the topic simply never came up. Michael was a dentist. His job was to keep his patients' teeth healthy. That's what he did. He had a successful practice. He provided a generous living for his family, who were all relatively healthy, Grizzy's challenges included.

But that's a problem, isn't it? If people like Michael are allowed to live good, successful lives, then how will the rest of us ever learn our lesson?

Michael woke suddenly in the darkness, his body alert. Alert about what?

A broken window.

Panther was barking viciously downstairs. Michael leapt out of bed, stumbling in the covers, and flipped on the light switch.

"Get the kids into the panic room!" he told Kate. Then, rushing to his dresser, he pulled out his gun and grabbed the box of bullets.

Panther was still barking. He had never heard her so wild—growling, snarling. Good old girl. Michael's hands trembled as he tried to remember how to release the cylinder. His fingers fumbled. Why isn't Kate moving yet? There! The cylinder slid to the side and he tried to load the first bullet. His fingers wouldn't cooperate. Panther continued her frenzied barking. Keep them busy, girl. He loaded the first bullet. Why isn't Kate moving?

"Kate—" Michael turned and looked at the empty bed. Where's Kate? Then he realized: She's downstairs on the couch with Grizzy.

Michael dropped a bullet. The box was shaking in his hand. Cursing, he grabbed another. Panther was still barking. He loaded a second bullet.

A loud bang shook the floor. The barking stopped.

"You bastard!" No time to finish loading, Michael slammed the cylinder into place.

Kate and Grizzy are downstairs!

Michael flew out of the room and raced down the stairs. Reaching the bottom, he glanced toward the kitchen before hurriedly creeping to the hallway. Holding his revolver in front of him, he moved toward the family room. The shooter must be in the kitchen. How long before he moves to the front room?

Michael stopped where the hallway wall ended, the front room opening to his left, the family room to his right. Both were dark, although there was a small light from the kitchen. Glancing quickly, he thought he saw a shadow move within it. He turned back to the family room.

"Kate," Michael hissed. "Kate, are you down here?"

There was a low noise, like a recorded voice, coming from behind the couch.

"Kate!" Michael whispered louder. He peeked again around the wall. The shadow in the kitchen was nearing the entrance to the front room.

Kate's head popped up. Her face was white and she had a phone to her ear.

Smart woman, Michael thought. She called the police.

Then he heard footsteps enter the front room—slow, intentional footsteps. He remembered the saying: "When seconds count, the police are only minutes away."

"I have a gun!" Michael shouted. Kate's eyes widened as she realized what he was holding. He motioned for her and Grizzy to move into the hallway with him.

"I have a gun! Get out of my house!" he yelled.

There was no reply, but the footsteps stopped. Michael stood with his back against the wall, his revolver held in both hands, pointed at the ceiling. He peeked quickly around the corner but saw nothing. Kate and Grizzy were crawling over from the couch. They seemed to take forever. Then they were there, Kate crouching on the ground beside Grizzy, who was trembling. Kate still had the phone up to her ear.

"He's in our front room," she whispered. "No, we haven't seen him yet. Yes, it might be a woman. We don't know. Yes, they have a gun." Her voice cracked at this and she looked up at the gun that Michael held in his hands. Grizzy leaned against Kate. She seemed on the verge of a panic attack. Michael felt like he might join her.

The footsteps started moving again, coming further into the front room. That meant the shooter was moving away from the stairs.

"Get up into the panic room," Michael whispered to Kate. "Grab Tank. Get in the panic room and bar the door."

Kate glanced at the stairs and then back at Michael. He could guess her thoughts. If the shooter is in the front room, she and Grizzy would be exposed as soon as they stepped past the hallway wall.

"I'll distract him," Michael whispered, motioning with his gun. "Now, go!"

Kate started to move, dragging Grizzy behind her. Michael heard something fall to the ground in the hallway but he was turning into the front room, his gun held out in front of him, his finger shaking on the trigger.

Then he saw the shooter and he froze. The man was standing there in the middle of the front room, staring right back at him, a gun in his hand. It was shocking how ordinary the man looked. Michael had expected something dramatic—He broke into my house! He shot Panther!—but the person standing there could have been anyone. Except for his eyes. Michael saw the anger and hatred that burned within them. Those eyes didn't see a man when they looked at Michael. Those eyes could see nothing more than a bigot, a monster that must be destroyed for righteousness' sake. How can anyone allow themselves to be filled with such irrational anger?

There was running in the hallway as Kate and Grizzy made a break for the stairs. The shooter's gun turned toward them and Michael yelled, "No!" as he pointed his shaking revolver at the man and pulled the trigger.

It clicked but didn't fire. He pulled the trigger again and again and again. Click, click, click. The shooter heard the dry fires and was swinging his gun back toward Michael. Bang! Michael's revolver went off, Michael's eyes closing instinctively at the loud noise, and the bullet flew wild. The shooter had his gun pointed back at Michael, who pulled the trigger again. Another blast. He ducked behind the wall as the shooter returned fire, their downstairs filling with terrible blasts. Michael could smell the smoke. His stomach churned. He wanted to vomit.

"Think about what you're doing!" he yelled, his voice sounding hoarse. He glanced up the stairs. At least Kate and Grizzy had made it. He heard a low sound coming from the ground. Looking down, he saw the phone Kate had dropped in her flight to the stairs. He couldn't understand what the operator was saying.

"Think about what you're doing!" Michael yelled again. "Are you going to kill me for having a different opinion?"

"Opinion!" the shooter roared, and Michael recognized his voice from all those phone calls. "Opinion! This isn't about your opinion! This is about your money! You paid to take rights away from others. You paid! This isn't about your opinion, you bigoted Nazi!"

"Rights?" Michael asked, shocked at the man's words. He killed Panther for this? He's shooting at me for this? "What rights?" Michael asked, his back against the wall. "You and I are both men. You and I have the exact same rights!" Then he crouched low as the shooter growled and fired a shot through the wall where his head had been. Michael saw where the bullet had pierced the opposite wall.

"You stole their right to marry who they love!" the shooter yelled. "You paid to take their families away from them! Now I'm going to take your family away from you! No one has the right to steal the rights of another! You stole their right to marry who they love!"

If person A loves person B, will you always say yes? I doubt that, Michael thought.

"Love is love!" the shooter yelled, his gun blasting a hole above Michael's head, the bullet striking a picture of Michael's family that hung on the opposite wall, the picture's glass shattering and falling to the floor. Michael dropped to his hands and knees on the ground.

"Love is love!" the shooter screamed again, his bullet striking lower this time, but Michael had crawled toward the staircase. He'd have to make a break for it. But that would leave him exposed.

Michael held his empty gun in his hand. He wondered how many bullets the shooter had left. His ears rung from the sound of gunfire. *I need to make it to the panic room*, he thought. *I don't want to die in flannel pajamas.*

Rising to a crouch, Michael threw his gun behind him into the family room. It knocked over a vase with a loud crash. He darted toward the stairs.

"Bigot!" the shooter yelled a second later. "You won't get away from this, bigot!"

Michael heard footsteps running after him. He raced up the stairs and flew around the corner. The panic room was ahead of him. Kate's tear-filled face was peeking out.

"Move!" Michael yelled as he barreled toward it.

The shooter's feet were pounding up the stairs. "Homophobe!" the shooter screamed.

Michael burst into the panic room, almost running over Kate, who stood behind the doorway. He flung the metal door shut, slamming the bar into place just as fists started pounding on the door.

"I hate how hateful you are!" the shooter shrieked, and the room filled with large thuds as he rammed his body against the door.

"I hate how hateful you are!" the shooter shrieked again. He struck the door repeatedly with both hands and feet.

Tank was whimpering on the ground, Kate hugging him tight, Grizzy kneeling next to them. Michael stood and watched the door. It's steel, Michael reminded himself. He can't hurt us now.

The shooter grew silent, and the only sound was Grizzy's hurried whispering. Michael looked down at her, worried she might be having a panic attack. She was praying. At least I taught her one thing right, Michael said to himself. Then he turned his attention back to the door, wondering what the shooter was up to.

"Michael."

Michael jumped at the whisper from under the door. Somehow the fact that the shooter knew his name shocked him even more than being shot at. Of course he knows my name, Michael reminded himself. It was plastered all over the Internet along with the rest of the Proposition 8 donors.

"Michael," the whisper came again.

He must be lying down right in front of the door, Michael thought.

"Michael, I'm sorry about your dog."

Michael turned and looked at Kate, who stared back wide eyed. Of all the crazy things—

A gunshot echoed through the room, followed by a thud on the ground outside.

"Did he just—" Kate's voice caught. Tank was blubbering more than before. Grizzy didn't stop praying.

"I think so," Michael said. He put his ear up to the door. He couldn't hear anything. "I should check."

"The police are coming," Kate said.

"Are you sure?" Michael asked.

Kate buried her face in Tank's thick shoulder.

The shooter is probably dead, Michael thought. He was probably planning a murder-suicide, and with murder impossible, he switched to just suicide. Michael wished he had his gun still. Looking around the small room, he looked for a weapon, but the food cans didn't seem very useful.

Then he saw his old golf clubs. Reaching into the bag, he took out his favorite putter. Then, turning back to the door, he lifted the metal bar out of the way and slowly pulled the door open.

"Michael, don't!" Kate yelled and sprang to her feet.

But Michael had already peeked out from behind the doorway. And there was the shooter, standing with his gun pointed right back at Michael, the shooter's eyes an inferno. "Bigots don't deserve to be happy!"

The shooter fired, Kate pulling Michael back into the panic room right before the bullet struck the door frame. And suddenly the hallway was filled with voices—"Freeze! Drop the gun!"—followed by gunfire. "He's down! He's down!"

Michael collapsed onto his knees. Kate was there beside him. He wrapped his arms around his wife and children, tears of fear and relief running down his face. Grizzy never stopped praying.

▷   ◁

Detective Price stepped through the front door and looked around the room, pulling out his notebook and beginning to jot down details for the investigation. There was a nice little gunfight here, he thought. The bullet marks were prominent in the wall that divided the front room from the hallway. A few pictures had been shattered, a vase too, and the smell of gunpowder lingered in the room. Turning his attention away from the bullet holes, the detective looked up at a large oil painting that hung in the center of the wall. I'll bet that cost a bundle, he thought. It was some sort of church building, perhaps a cathedral or a temple. Beside it hung a framed document: "The Family: A Proclamation to the World." Detective Price shrugged and walked into the kitchen, where a couple of officers were looking down at a dead German shepherd.

"It's a shame about the dog," an officer said. "They're beautiful animals. Loyal, too."

Detective Price jotted down some details from the kitchen. There was a broken pane of glass on the kitchen door. That was how the shooter must have entered. "Have we ID'd the shooter?" the detective asked.

"Not yet," an officer responded.

"And who'd he try to kill?"

"Michael Keeler."

"Michael Keeler? Where have I heard that name before?"

"He's a Prop 8 donor. Gave $1,000."

The detective paused, turning to the officer in surprise. Then he snorted and put away his pen and notebook. "Well, I guess the bigot just got what was coming to him, didn't he?"

The Equality Remedy

ON THE CORNER OF BEAUTY AND TRAN-
quility, nestled half an acre behind a vast green
hedge, lay the fairy castle, the home of Mother Nature herself and countless cheerful fairies. Greg the mailman loved
to deliver mail there. It was the highlight of his route. He
always saved it until the very end because no matter how
many dogs had chased him or snotty kids had thrown
mud balls at him, just seeing the grounds of the castle and
speaking to the fairies always drove any unpleasant feelings away.

He could already feel the peace settling into his body
as he turned the corner onto Beauty and headed toward
Tranquility. The sky seemed to be bluer the further he
drove, the grass greener. He could hear birds chirping
through the open door of his mail truck, and the flowers—
oh, the flowers—the flowers were indescribable.

With a sigh of pleasure, he turned into the small driveway that led to the fairy mailbox, the driveway indented a
little into the hedge wall itself. As always, there were fairies there waiting for him, and as always, Greg the mailman
felt guilty he only had junk mail to deliver.

No one thanks Mother Nature. How often do we stand under a clear blue sky, lift our arms up in the air, and shout, "Thank you!" Never. We never do that. No one thanks Mother Nature, so the only mail she ever got was junk mail.

Greg the mailman parked the car, grabbed today's junk, and walked up to the two fairies, one red and one blue, that hovered next to the mailbox.

"Did we get a lot of fan mail today?" the blue fairy asked.

"Same as always," Greg the mailman replied. Actually, it was just two credit card offers and an advertisement from a dentist, but he never had the heart to tell them the truth. They always assumed every bit of mail was fan mail.

"They love us!" the red fairy said, eagerly grabbing the dental advertisement, a dentist's wife and kids smiling professionally on the ad between the red fairy's hugging arms. "They really love us!"

The blue fairy seized the credit card offers in the same manner. Greg the mailman smiled. Hey, if it makes them so happy, what does it hurt to not tell them the truth? he said to himself. Then he frowned when he heard what sounded like distant shouting.

"Hey, hey, ho, ho …"

He lifted an ear in the direction but couldn't make out more than the first few words.

"Hey, hey, ho, ho …"

"What's that yelling?" he asked the fairies.

"It's our fans!" the fairies erupted in unison. "They came to cheer for us! They're so wonderful! Our fans have come to see us!"

Greg the mailman scratched his chin. "Those don't sound like fans," he said, noting the harsh tone to the "hey's" and the "ho's."

"Come see!" the blue fairy said. "Come see our fans!" The blue fairy flew into the hedge, the bushes leaning to each side to provide an entrance. Greg the mailman followed, in awe at being within the fairy compound. And there, atop a small hill, lay the fairy castle. Made of wood, made of stone, made of flower, Greg the mailman couldn't tell, but it seemed to bloom up out of the ground. And there was Mother Nature herself, looking out a second-story window. She wore a dark yellow dress and her hair was raised up in a pattern as wild as a tree's branches. Greg the mailman had never seen a more beautiful woman in his life. *The* woman. That's what she was: *the* woman. In all his years delivering mail, he had only seen her a handful of times, but there she was, leaning out of the window and talking to the birds who fluttered around her chirping happily. Then she waved at him. Greg the mailman's heart skipped a beat. Mother Nature was waving at him! Sheepishly, he removed his hat and waved in return, her attention warming him and making him feel two decades younger. Then he stumbled over a goat.

"What?" he sputtered, his face in the grass. "Who put that goat there?"

He stood up, dusting off his pants and shirt before glancing nervously back up at the castle, worried that Mother Nature had seen him fall. The window was empty. Then he turned back to the goat, which was munching on the hedge. Stupid goat, he thought, tempted to kick it.

But the blue fairy and the red fairy were flying there, blissful grins on their faces, so Greg the mailman returned his hat to his head and turned toward the hedge as the blue fairy parted it.

"See, our fans!" the blue fairy said.

Greg the mailman looked through the hole in the hedge at the most unhappy group of protesters he had ever seen. They were all waving signs, most of which cannot be reprinted here, and they were glaring and they were chanting, and Greg the mailman could finally hear what they were saying.

"Hey, hey, ho, ho, heteronormativity has got to go! Hey, hey, ho, ho, heteronormativity has got to go!"

"It's not a very catchy cheer," the blue fairy said, looking disappointed.

The red fairy furrowed miniature brows. "What is heteronormativity?"

"I think it's another word for reality," the blue fairy replied.

This cheered the red fairy, who spun in a circle and said: "Foolish humans, they say the silliest things when they're bored!"

The blue fairy fluttered in front of Greg the mailman's face. "What do you think about our fans' cheer?"

"I think it's rubbish," Greg the mailman said, disgusted at the whole display.

"Rubbish?" the goat said, raising its head. "I like rubbish."

"Oh, shut up, you old goat," Greg the mailman said.

"Sure, be mean to the goat," the goat said. "No one cares what a goat feels. No one cares what a goat thinks."

Then the goat went back to its munching and Greg the mailman went back to watching the protesters outside of the hedge.

This is worse than the junk mail, he thought. This is actually dangerous. To have this level of negativity so close to the fairy castle ... The protesters might do something stupid, or worse, the protesters might make the fairies angry, and if the fairies become angry, and if one of them curses ... Well, everyone knows that when a fairy curses, they lose all their magic, and when they lose all their magic, just like that, they're gone.

"Let's close the hedge and talk about this for a minute," Greg the mailman said.

With a flap of blue fairy wings, the hedge was back in place, the protest chant once again muted.

"Those aren't fans," Greg the mailman explained. "Those are protesters."

"Protesters!" the blue fairy said. "Why would there be protesters here? Are they bored? Humans do silly things when they're bored."

"I don't know," Greg the mailman said. "But it's not good. It's not good at all."

The red fairy laughed. "Oh, we're not worried about a few ornery humans! What will they do, send goblins and ogres against us?"

"Worse," Greg the mailman said. "Lawyers."

▷ ◁

And, unfortunately, Greg the mailman was right. Not more than two days later, a court summons came, and Mother Nature herself was called to stand before the court. Greg the mailman was there, fighting for an open seat with the humans and the fairy-tale creatures. They all stood when Mother Nature walked into the room, Mother Nature wearing a long green velvet dress that trailed on the ground behind her, plants blooming out of the carpet in her wake, her hair rising high above her head, a small green bird perched inside it, chirping away a happy tune. Father Time went beside her, his long white beard almost touching the floor, the current year written on a sash he wore over his chest. He would serve as her representative in the proceedings. The two of them took their places at the front of the courtroom. And then the human lawyer entered the room, a hush passing over the crowd as they eyed his perfectly manicured suit and magnificent mullet. There was something distinctly reptilian about him. No, not reptilian: amphibian. The sliminess seemed to ooze off him as he walked up the aisle, the lawyer grinning from ear to ear; and the hand of every man in the room reached instinctively to protect their wallets.

Then, the lawyer and defendant in place, the judge entered the room. Everyone stood as he shambled to his desk. He was a strange-looking fellow, like a cross between the Grim Reaper and the Sandman. Seeing such a being on the bench, Greg the mailman had no idea what to expect from the proceedings. But it all started with the lawyer standing up and laying out the case against Mother Nature.

"We are here today to bring vile charges against Mother Nature," the lawyer said, strolling up in front of the judge. "Mother Nature is hereby charged with the horrible crime of heteronormativity."

The lawyer whirled and looked at her. "Furthermore, I charge that she is an unruly dresser and just a bad, bad person in general." He raised a finger and pointed it at her. "Heterosexist! Heterosexist!"

The crowd burst into shouting, the small green bird perched within Mother Nature's hair chirping obscenely at the lawyer. Then the judge banged his gavel. "Order!" he shouted. "I want order!"

A stranger sitting next to Greg the mailman leaned over and whispered, "What's heteronormativity?"

Greg the mailman leaned over in return and whispered, "I think it's another word for reality."

"Oh, okay," the stranger nodded and sat back up. Greg the mailman sat up too.

Then the stranger leaned over again. "Why are we putting reality on trial?"

Greg the mailman thought about this for a moment. To him the answer was obvious: electricity. Surely this level of hubris had only been reached after fermenting for years under the corrupting comfort of artificial lights. But Greg the mailman didn't share this insight, afraid the stranger might think him a Luddite, with their worship of dark city streets, nonfunctional pacemakers, and melted ice cream. Instead Greg the mailman decided to take a more philosophical approach and he whispered: "Because we're humans."

"Ah, of course," the stranger said, sitting up straight again. "How could I have forgotten that?"

Then the stranger sprang up on top of his chair, raised a fist into the air, and shouted, "Down with cabbage and all its dark deeds!"

The stranger waited expectantly, fist held high, but the courtroom paid him no mind. Glaring at the crowd, he jumped down and stomped out of the room, muttering that tomatoes were a vegetable and he didn't care if anyone said otherwise. The courtroom door closed behind him.

Then Father Time rose to face the lawyer, who still stood pointing a finger at Mother Nature. Father Time launched into a forceful, persuasive argument, citing precedent, complaining about jurisdiction. He skated around the lawyer—no, really, he was wearing golden roller skates—and made mincemeat of the lawyer's accusations, his words riling up the courtroom crowd. A man in the first row was so excited he tried to get the wave going, but no one else paid him any attention, so he stomped out of the courtroom following after the stranger.

The lawyer was taken back, dizzied by Father Time's swift circles around his position. He begged for a month recess, which the judge granted with a bang of his gavel.

➤   ◄

The fairy castle brimmed with joy at how well the first day of the trial had gone. The protesters were still outside, the air full of their constant chanting: "Hey, hey, ho, ho, heteronormativity has got to go!" But as the month past, the fairies paid them no mind because Greg the mailman kept bringing them junk mail, which they thought was fan mail; and thinking it was fan mail, they assumed that most everyone was on their side.

"See, they want Mother Nature to win!" the red fairy said, clutching an HVAC ad. "Not all humans are silly! Not all humans are bored!"

Greg the mailman was happy to see them happy, but he felt apprehensive about the trial. There was something in the eye of the lawyer after the judge granted the month recess. It made Greg the mailman worried.

And he was right to be worried. Once the recess was over and they found themselves back in court again, everyone realized how sneaky the lawyer had been when he asked for a month recess. Now it was January and rather than Father Time walking beside Mother Nature, Baby Time waddled there instead, constantly tripping over the sash he wore around his neck and sucking on a pacifier.

This doesn't look good, Greg the mailman thought.

It didn't go good, either. Gone was the forceful eloquence of Father Time, gone were his golden roller skates and his swift circles around the lawyer. The impact was obvious during jury selection. Although the jury pool was mostly human, there was a healthy sprinkling of mythological creatures as well: a minotaur in khaki shorts, a couple of dryads, some leprechauns, a towering treant, a political centrist.

Greg the mailman figured that as long as some of the mythological creatures got selected for the jury, Mother Nature would have a decent shot. But one by one they were all eliminated from the jury pool along with every one of the reasonable-looking humans. Greg the mailman was depressed to see the nine jurors left to decide the case, each one of them puny in stature. Not puny physically, but puny mentally. It chilled him to hear the nine runts murmuring the word "privilege" back and forth like some sort of religious rite. He didn't know what it meant, but he assumed such superstition wasn't good news for Mother Nature.

The amphibianish lawyer strutted to the front of the courtroom, the back of his mullet trailing party-like over the collar of his checkered suit jacket. Turning around dramatically, he lifted up his tie for the crowd to see.

"Do you see my tie, ladies and gentlemen?" he asked. "Do you see what color it is? It's black. For those of you who are color-blind, I'm telling you right now, it's black."

The lawyer paused, seeming to listen to the crowd, although no one was talking. "What's that you ask?" he said. "You want to know why I'm wearing a black tie? Okay, I'll tell you."

His face sagged, his eyes becoming wet with tears. "I'm wearing a black tie because I'm in mourning." Another pause. "What am I mourning? I'm glad you asked. I'll tell you."

Then he drew himself up straight, his face becoming hard and his eyes focusing on Mother Nature. "I'm mourning injustice," he said. "Injustice, unfairness, inequality, discrimination. That's why I'm mourning, ladies and gentlemen. That's why I'm wearing a black tie."

Suddenly full of energy, he strode to the jury box. "Look back in history, ladies and gentlemen. Look back decades, centuries, millennia. What do you see? Throughout all human history, what has been the one constant? A generation comes, followed by another, followed by another, followed by another. Generation after generation after generation. And what has been the constant through all those generations?"

He paused to catch his breath. "The constant, ladies and gentlemen, has been male-female couples. Each generation that was born was there because of male-female couples. Each generation would *not* have been there had it not been for male-female couples. Throughout time and history, male-female couples have been important, have been necessary, have been essential. But I ask you this, ladies and gentlemen, is that fair?"

The lawyer pounded the wall of the jury box. "No! Ladies and gentlemen, no, it's not! It's not fair. It's inequality! It's discrimination! Why must male-female couples be so important? Why must they be superior to all other couples?"

He turned away from the jury, walking in front of the courtroom to face the audience. "Oh, I know, I know. Some will say it's just reality that makes male-female couples superior. Some will say it's just nature. And to that, ladies and gentlemen, I reply: YES!"

He pointed an accusing finger at Mother Nature. "It's because nature—it's because Mother Nature herself—is heterosexist!"

A shocked gasp ran through the jury.

"She is!" the lawyer continued. "She is! She's heterosexist and now it's time for her male-female-couple-preferring tyranny to end!"

What rubbish, Greg the mailman thought, sitting stiffly in his chair, his arms tightly folded. What complete rubbish.

"We are here to charge Mother Nature with the vilest of discrimination," the lawyer continued, walking back to the jury box. "Her so-called natural model of procreation unfairly prefers male-female couples, conferring an inherent superiority to them over all other combinations. This heterosexism must be abolished! We have big dreams, ladies and gentlemen. We have big plans of how to remold civilization into a more just and a more egalitarian model. We demand that Mother Nature stop interfering with those plans! Reality must no longer be allowed to play favorites. Reality must no longer be allowed to stand in our way!"

On and on the lawyer went, browbeating the jury, the courtroom, the judge. Greg the mailman looked around at the cowed crowd and wished that someone would say something about cabbages. Only Mother Nature looked unfazed, sitting there calmly with both hands resting upon the table, one hand on top of the other. But the rest of the crowd was swaying along with the lawyer who continued his rant against nature. And, listening to the lawyer, Greg the mailman felt ashamed of his own humanity. If ever he had wished to have been born a squirrel—and he often had—he definitely wished it now. Not some stupid, fat squirrel that scrambles around park benches picking up table scraps, but a flying squirrel, able to leap from tall tree to tall tree. That way he would be cute and fluffy, plus he could fly, plus he could bite any snotty kid that came too close and no one would object at all because, hey, he's just a squirrel.

Greg the mailman became lost in his squirrel dream, feeling the wind beneath him as he soared through the air, so he missed the lawyer's summation. But Greg the mailman's attention returned when Baby Time stumbled forward and began a rambling, whiny defense, followed by a temper tantrum in front of the judge. Greg the mailman thought Baby Time did an okay job for someone who had only learned to speak days ago, but the presentation simply couldn't hold up against someone as skilled and slimy as the lawyer. And with such intellectual giants in the jury box, the verdict was a foregone conclusion. Still, Greg the mailman couldn't help feeling shock as he heard the ruling read by the judge.

Mother Nature was ruled to be a miserable heterosexist. Furthermore, the court ruled that the male-female nature of procreation was irrational and prejudiced. In addition, it was a clear violation of the equal protection of mumbo jumbo and the iron pantaloons.

(That last part had everyone scratching their heads, unsure if perhaps the jury had poor handwriting or if the judge had just decided to improvise and end on a rhetorical flourish.)

Baby Time had been successful on one point, however. He had been able to wring out a concession as part of the verdict that the remedy itself would be decided solely by Mother Nature. The jury had agreed to this requirement, knowing that only Mother Nature truly understood nature and therefore only she could remold it according to their dictates.

The protesters all cheered the verdict. No longer would male-female couples be more important than other combinations. The tyranny of nature had been brought to heel. Reality itself would now bend to popular sentiment. It was a good day for bored humans, a good day for bored humans everywhere. Each and every one of them stayed up late that night, partying incoherently underneath the shallow brilliance of their artificial lights.

▷   ◁

The fairies stared at Mother Nature in disbelief after she made the change. How could Mother Nature do such a horrible thing? Yes, the humans were silly. Yes, they were arrogant. But to take something beautiful and to replace it with this ... It just felt wrong, so very wrong.

Mother Nature herself mourned what she had done. Dressed all in gray, her hair fell flat down her sides and back, her face pale, her skin cold. No birds chirped around her. None could bear the sight of the tears on her cheeks.

"It is what they demanded," Mother Nature said, her face falling into her hands.

But as the blue fairy looked out the castle window at the world and perceived what the world had become, the blue fairy felt bitterness; and the bitterness grew and grew until, unthinking, the blue fairy slammed a hand down hard on the windowsill and blurted out, "What a load of horse—"

And, just like that, they were gone.

➤ ◄

Greg the mailman was sitting in his recliner that night when his wife walked into the room wearing lingerie, a flimsy, shiny red thing he always loved to see her in. (His wife didn't know he dreamed of being a squirrel. She always thought of him more as a raccoon.)

But, watching his wife sway her hips into the room, Greg the mailman realized a peculiar thing. He looked down at his trousers, back up at his wife in her lingerie, and then back down at his trousers again. Well, that's interesting, he thought.

And what was more peculiar, his wife wasn't upset at all. She hadn't been in the mood anyway. It was his night, so she had dressed for it, but if he wasn't in the mood either, she wasn't going to complain.

The couple found themselves lying in bed next to each other, his wife still wearing her barely-there outfit, her reading glasses on, with a large book open on her lap. Greg the mailman lay on his back and stared up at the ceiling. He was surprised his wife was reading a biography. She always reads romance novels, he said to himself. I wonder what changed her mind tonight? Then he gasped at a sudden pain in his side.

"What's wrong?" his wife asked without looking up from her book.

"I don't know," Greg the mailman said, rubbing his side. It didn't hurt anymore, but was that a lump he could feel there?

And the lump grew, every day a little larger. Others were developing them too, always on the left side, always right below the rib cage. And, although no one cared enough to talk about it, it seemed as if everyone else had lost their interest in each other as well. At first no one thought about the source—if they didn't care, then they didn't care—but as the lumps on their sides grew larger, someone finally mentioned that perhaps this was the remedy Mother Nature had been forced to impose.

A few made the trek to the fairy castle to ask Mother Nature what was going on, but they were shocked to find the castle no longer there. Beauty was overgrown by poison ivy. Tranquility had become a cesspool. The goat was still there, munching on a huge pile of junk mail and the rubbish the protesters had left behind. But no one bothered asking the goat its opinion.

Months later, Greg the mailman lay in bed next to the Greg-the-mailman-sized lump growing out of his side. Then it happened. There was a sharp jerk, a slight tearing of the flesh, and the lump fell away, its skin rapidly falling apart, leaving Greg the mailman to look at a man lying on the bed next to him, a man who looked just like him. Greg the mailman raised his head and looked down his clone's naked body, where he noticed one profound difference. Then Greg the mailman lay his head back down and looked into the eyes of his sex-less clone. Speaking in unison, they said, "What a pile of horse—"

And, just like that, we were gone.

Talents, Servants, and Government Busybodies

AMASTER HAD THREE SERVANTS. HE GAVE the first servant five talents, the second servant two talents, and the third servant one talent. Then the master went away for a time, leaving his servants to look after themselves and what they had been given.

And the first servant, who had been given five talents, worked hard, doubling his five talents to ten. And the second servant, who had been given two talents, worked hard as well, doubling her two talents to four. But the third servant did not work hard. He did not work at all. He buried his talent in the ground instead, where it lay wasted and unused.

When the master returned from his journey, he sought an account of how his servants had fared. The first servant reported he had taken the five talents he had been given and had earned five more. The second servant reported she had taken the two talents she had been given and had earned two more. The third servant reported he had buried his talent in the ground and had earned nothing.

And the master, knowing what behaviors he wanted to encourage and what behaviors he wanted to discourage, rewarded those servants who had doubled their talents, but the servant who had hidden his talent the master rewarded not. Instead, the master took the talent away from the unproductive servant and gave it to the servant who had earned five.

But then the government busybodies intruded into the story. From the servant who had gained two talents, the government busybodies taxed one talent. From the servant who had gained six talents (five earned and one awarded), the government busybodies taxed four. And then the government busybodies, congratulating themselves for their generosity, took the talents they had confiscated and redistributed them to the talentless servant, who promptly buried them in the ground, where they were lost forever.

And the reader comprehends the parable, looks at the world outside, and says: "We are so screwed."

The Mascot

ONE WALL OF THE PRINCIPAL'S OFFICE WAS filled from floor to ceiling with trophies and awards. Merit scholarships, sports championships, debate victories, band accomplishments, all locked behind a pane of glass. The light dim, Winston stepped closer to get a better look, ignoring his vague reflection in the glass. It was incredible how successful Ocean High was. That's the reason he had chosen to enroll there. That's the reason he stood there now in their principal's office, backpack stuffed full of books, black trumpet case in hand.

He could have signed up for an online school. His mother had almost encouraged it, feeling guilty about the move that forced Winston to change schools the middle of his junior year. The move wasn't her fault, of course. It wasn't his dad's fault either. It just was. People get laid off. Kids have to change schools. It happens. You deal with it and you move on.

Yes, he could have signed up for an online school, but everyone spoke so highly of Ocean High, and seeing the wall of accomplishments, Winston was beginning to understand why. He looked at a football trophy, five years old, the faceless boy on the top holding a ball in one hand as he held out the other to ward off tackles. Ocean High had won the championship every year for the last decade. Faceless boy after faceless boy perched atop trophy after trophy.

No one ever transferred away from Ocean High; that's what everyone said, and that must be good, right? It was the main feeder school for all the state universities. Rumor was any student from Ocean High who wanted to attend college would automatically be granted admission. That's how good it was. The college spokesmen all said that students from Ocean High made perfect college students because they arrived already thinking exactly how a college student is expected to think.

Probably an exaggeration, Winston thought, unable to understand how everyone in a school could be expected to think and act the same way.

To the right of the trophies hung various scholarly awards. Someone had won the national spelling bee. Winston looked at the picture attached to the plaque, a smiling girl with blonde hair. She seemed pretty, but there was something odd about her, something a little bit … off. Winston leaned in closer. Was it just a trick of the glass?

A woman's face appeared suddenly in the glass next to him, causing Winston to jump back. Feeling silly, he turned to face the woman, Principal Malter, gray hair and thick glasses. She smiled as she held out a paper.

"Here's your schedule," she said. "We were able to find a spot for you in the band. I'm sure you'll enjoy it."

Winston took the paper eagerly. Joining the band had been the main reason he had wanted to enroll here. Like everything else, Ocean High had the best band, and now he would be a part of it. It was an exciting thought, but also an intimidating one. Would he be good enough to win any parts? Or would he always be far back in the pack of other trumpet players?

"Thank you," he told her.

She stood and watched him, the side of her face reflected in the glass pane to her right.

"Are we in the middle of class time right now?" Winston asked, feeling nervous at her attention. He didn't like to be stared at, especially by adults.

"For some," Principal Malter replied. "Others have lunch right now."

"How about me?" Winston asked. He looked down at his schedule, eager for an excuse to look away from her.

"Oh, we have a student coming to show you around," she said, which didn't really answer his question. She was still watching him.

"Okay, I'll just wait out in the foyer," Winston told her, but as he started to turn toward the door, she grabbed his shoulder and held him in place.

"Ocean High has the right sort of students, Winston." she told him, the smile still on her face. "The right sort of students who think the right sort of things." Her grip tightened on his shoulder as her gaze intensified.

What is she looking for? Winston worried. Is there something wrong with me? I just want to play in the band.

"Are you the right sort of student, Winston?" she asked. "Do you think the right sort of things?"

Winston didn't know how to reply. He didn't know what she meant. She raised one of her eyebrows and continued to stare at him, not smiling anymore.

"Umm …" he said. But then the door to the office opened and a boy walked in, taking the principal's attention away from Winston.

"Ah, Gary," she said. "I was just explaining our school to Winston here. It's a great school, isn't it, Gary?"

"Of course," the boy replied, his hands in the front pockets of trendy jeans.

The principal's grip loosened on Winston's shoulder and she took a step back. Winston let out the breath he'd been holding.

"Please show Winston around the school," the principal said.

"Of course," the boy replied again. "Follow me," he told Winston as he turned back out the door.

"Oh, one more thing, Gary," Principal Malter said.

"Yes?" Gary said, turning his head back to look at her.

"Make sure you show him Room E."

"Of course," he said. Then he looked back at Winston. "Follow me," he repeated.

Winston hurried after Gary, eager to be away from the principal and her odd statements and her odd staring. The right sort of student? What was that supposed to mean?

Gary waved his arm at the foyer.

"This is the foyer," he said.

"Okay," Winston replied. There were a couple of large steps in the far corner against the wall, where a group of jocks huddled to one side, a cluster of cheerleaders sitting next to them. They all wore letterman jackets.

"Does the band get letterman jackets?" Winston asked.

"Of course, but they never wear them to school, of course."

"Oh," Winston said, disappointed.

"The cafeteria is through those doors," Gary said, pointing at them. "And that is the main entrance, of course," he said, pointing the other way.

There were two hallways that opened into the foyer. Gary led Winston toward one.

"This is the way to the band room," he said.

Winston followed after, giving a passing glance to the cool kids on the steps of the foyer. The cheerleaders were all beautiful, clearly out of his league. The jocks looked big, larger than he was used to. Do they do steroids at this school? he wondered. Is that why they always win?

A jock looked up, his dark flattop reminding Winston of a bully from junior high. Winston looked away, afraid to make eye contact. I'm sure things will be different here, he told himself. But he couldn't shake the feeling that Flattop was watching him as he left the foyer.

The hallway they entered felt too small, the ceiling shorter than normal, the walls tighter. Thankfully it was only half full, students wandering this way and that. Winston hated to think how crowded it could get when everyone was coming and going to class. The thought made him feel claustrophobic, but he brushed it aside. I'm sure it'll be fine, he told himself.

Gary stopped next to a closed door with a large glass window in the top.

"Here's the band room," he said. "The woodwinds are in class right now."

"They have a separate class?" Winston asked.

"Of course," Gary replied, raising an eyebrow. "Don't they always?"

"I don't know," Winston said. They hadn't at his last school. But his last school hadn't won any awards...

He looked through the window, unsurprised to see mainly girls filling the room; it was a woodwinds class after all. They all had their instruments to their lips, playing a single tone that sounded through the door—a single, constant, never-ending tone.

That's an odd way to practice, Winston thought. I wonder why they're doing that? Then he noticed two girls looking at him through the window, a pair of pretty, black-haired twins, one with a red bow in her hair and one with a pink. They both lowered their clarinets and smiled at him. Winston smiled back. This is going to be a great school! he said to himself before hurrying after Gary, who was already walking away.

I wonder how often the brass practices with the woodwinds, Winston was asking himself when Gary suddenly stopped, causing Winston to bump into him.

"Sorry," Winston mumbled, taking a step back.

"Hey," Gary said as he turned around to look at Winston, "do you want to meet our mascot? It's a unicorn!"

Winston was about to laugh. A unicorn? What kind of a silly joke is that? But then he noticed the look in Gary's eyes, a searching look, the same look Principal Malter had used. Is this some kind of initiation? Winston wondered. Some trick they like to play on their new students?

He decided to play along. "Okay," he told Gary. "Sounds good."

Gary nodded. "We keep it in Room E. It's right this way."

Winston followed after, shaking his head. This was the part of high school he hated. Shared jokes, shared enthusiasm, shared school spirit. Like some constant pep rally. It was annoying. He just wanted to play his trumpet, do good in school, and then leave. Well, and maybe date one of those cute clarinet twins. Or both of them. Winston smiled at the thought.

"Here it is," Gary said, stopping beside a door. This one had no window to see inside. Winston looked at the sign to the door's left: "EQUALITY." It was written entirely in uppercase, the text so large it seemed to be shouting. So this is Room E? Winston thought. What a strange school.

Students continued to pass back and forth. None seemed to be paying any attention to him, which was good. Having to participate in a school joke was one thing, having everyone watch him be the butt of that joke was something else.

Gary smiled at Winston. "Here we are. Ready to see our unicorn?"

Winston smiled back. Play along, he told himself. "Of course," he said, mimicking Gary. The right sort of students, the principal said. If being the right sort of student will let me play my trumpet in the band and date the clarinet twins then I—

Gary turned the door knob and pushed. The door slowly opened, revealing a single chair in the middle of the room.

It looked like some sort of dentist's chair—a dentist's chair with straps on its arms. Well, that's a little disturbing, Winston thought; but then the door opened further, revealing their "unicorn."

Winston laughed. Okay, he thought. Stupid joke or not, I have to admit that's pretty funny.

But Gary stared silently at Winston. "Why are you laughing?" he asked, a penetrating look in his eyes.

Winston cocked his head and looked at the other student. "Listen," Winston said, "I might be new here, but I'm no freshman. I get the joke. It's funny. Your mascot is a unicorn. Ha ha."

In Room E, standing on four legs by the window and eating a potted plant, was a donkey, a real live donkey, with a cardboard tube duct-taped to its head.

Gary continued to stare at Winston. "Why are you laughing? That's our mascot. It's a unicorn."

Now he's taking it a bit too far, Winston thought. He pointed at the donkey. "No," he said. "That's a donkey with a cardboard tube duct-taped to its head. Like I said, funny. Ha ha ha."

"No," Gary said, sounding forceful. "Look again. It has four hooves. It has a horn. That makes it a unicorn."

Winston looked from the donkey to Gary. He can't be serious, Winston thought, can he? "Lots of things have four hooves," he said. "And you call that a real horn? It's a cardboard tube! I'm telling you: that's *not* a unicorn."

But Gary just increased his forcefulness. "Look again," he repeated. "You'll see that it's a unicorn. The right sort of students all see that it's a unicorn. Look again. I'm sure you don't really mean to say such hateful things."

Winston took another glance into Room E. All he saw was a donkey with a cardboard tube duct-taped to its head.

"Hateful?" he said to Gary. "Reality isn't hateful. Reality is reality, and reality is that that's not a unicorn!"

Gary stood up straight, sucking in his breath. There was a dangerous look in his eyes.

"That ... is ... a ... unicorn!" he said, speaking with weird tones and pauses as if he expected Winston to catch some hidden hint, but Winston was having none of it.

"No ... that ... is ... not!"

"That is a unicorn!" Gary repeated, almost shouting now. Students were beginning to stop and watch the spectacle. Winston felt embarrassed. Great way to meet everyone, he thought.

"Listen, Gary, I don't know what your problem is, but that's obviously not a unicorn. I'm telling you: two plus two will never be five, and a donkey with a cardboard tube duct-taped to its head will never be a unicorn!"

Gary's eyes widened and his face turned white. What a weirdo, Winston thought. But then Gary, standing straight, leaned his head back, pointed accusingly at Winston, and shrieked in a high-pitched voice: "BIGOT!"

Every student in the narrow hallway stopped and stared. The kid's crazy, Winston thought, feeling his face turn red at the unwanted attention from the rest of the students. Bigot? I'm just telling him what it really is. That's not a unicorn. That's a donkey with a cardboard tube duct-taped to its head!

Gary continued his shrieking, his finger pointed at Winston, his eyes bearing down on him.

"BIGOT!"

Great, Winston thought, just great. My first day of school and I give a classmate a nervous breakdown. Great start, Winston. You're sure going to make friends here.

There was a thud, followed by another thud and another. Surprised, Winston looked away from Gary at the students who surrounded him in the hallway, every one of them dropping their textbooks and bags to the floor.

What in the world?

There was a silent pause, and then every student straightened their backs, tilted back their heads, pointed at Winston, and shrieked in a high tone: "BIGOT!"

Winston covered his ears.

"BIGOT!"

They were all around him, staring, pointing, shrieking.

"BIGOT!"

What's going on?

"BIGOT!"

Their eyes looked murderous, every finger pointed at him.

"BIGOT!"

Then someone grabbed his backpack and the crowd surged in. Panicking, Winston tugged his backpack free and began to run toward the foyer.

"BIGOT!"

The shrieks followed after.

"BIGOT!"

Passing others in the hallway, Winston saw them stand straight and begin to point.

"BIGOT!"

He ran past the band room, students already coming out the doorway. The black-haired twins were there in the hall, backs straight, fingers pointed, shrieking at him, their red and pink bows quivering to the high-pitched tone: "BIGOT!"

Winston ran as fast as he could, making it to the foyer a moment before the mass of shrieking students. The jocks and cheerleaders were all standing in front of the foyer steps, and the administrators had exited the principal's office and were standing too, blocking the front entrance. Principal Malter was there with the rest, everyone staring at Winston. The shrieks had almost reached him from the hallway.

"They're crazy!" he panted, resting with his hands on his knees. "They showed me some donkey and claimed it was a unicorn and then—"

Everyone in the foyer—the jocks, the cheerleaders, the administrators—everyone straightened their backs, tilted back their heads, pointed, and shrieked: "BIGOT!"

"Oh, no," Winston said as they all moved forward, shrieking students exiting the cafeteria, administrators blocking the front entrance, those in the hallway behind about to reach him. He looked around quickly. Flattop and the rest of the jocks were almost to him. Looking above the pointing cheerleaders, he saw the other hallway. It was his best chance. He sprinted forward and, feeling like a complete douchebag for doing it, he swung his trumpet case like crazy, tumbling cheerleaders in all directions as he plowed through to the hallway beyond.

The crowd stumbled over the fallen cheerleaders and Winston was able to make a quick left into another hallway, which was empty. Knowing he had only seconds, he scanned the hall, finding a janitor closet to his left. He hurried inside and closed the door.

"BIGOT!" the shrieks filled the hallway, along with the sound of rushing feet as the entire crowd hurried past.

"I hate public school. I hate public school. I hate public school," Winston whimpered in the dark, his heart feeling ready to burst. Please don't look in the closet. Please don't look in the closet. Please don't look in the closet. Please don't look in the closet.

No one did. And a moment later, the hallway was silent.

I've got to get out of here, Winston told himself. He opened the door a crack and looked down the hallway. Empty. Silent. Opening it a little further, he peeked his head in the opposite direction.

No one was there.

Quickly, he left the closet and tiptoed across the hallway to an open classroom. He peeked his head into the room and then, seeing no one, hurried inside. There were two windows on the far wall. Sunlight shone through and he could see green grass beyond, the normality of the scene strange after the past few moments of insanity. Then he noticed the chalk board and he froze. The word "conform" was written over and over again, covering every inch.

"I thought this brainwashing BS wasn't supposed to start until college," he said. Then, mimicking Gary's voice, he mocked, "The right sort of students all see that it's a unicorn. The right sort of students all see that it's a unicorn." He grunted. "The right sort of students? Ha. More like weak-minded idiots. What a bunch of blind, bandwagon-following morons."

Even the cute clarinet twins, he thought, feeling regret. All the cool kids? Sure. They just follow the flow, no surprise there. But the cute twins? That was disappointing.

He hurried to a window, found the latch, and tried to turn it, but it was stuck and wouldn't move. For a moment he imagined the horde of shrieking students finding him trapped there in the room. What will they do to me? he wondered. Is that what the chair in Room E is for? He pulled harder and eventually the latch turned. Relieved, he opened the window, quietly dropped his backpack and trumpet case to the ground outside, and then scurried after.

Bushes lined the school on this side. He crouched low and picked up his things. "I hate public school. I hate public school. I hate public school," he whispered as he looked and listened for any sign of his shrieking classmates.

There was no sound.

Ahead of him was an open grass field, large enough to be a football field but unmarked, used for some other purpose. Past the grass field was the parking lot. If I can just make it to the parking lot, then I can hide among the cars and sneak out the gate, he thought.

He took a deep breath and then started jogging across the grass, but something back at the building caught his eye. There, poking its head out an open window, was the donkey, noisily chewing on the bushes outside. It must have knocked its cardboard "horn" as it reached its head through the window, because now the tube hung to one side, the duct tape almost falling off.

"Oh, come on!" Winston said, stopping to look. "The duct tape is starting to come off! Look at it! It's a donkey! Just look! That's not a unicorn!"

The grass all around Winston began to ripple.

What's going on? he asked himself. He tried to step back, but his foot got caught. Looking down, he saw a hand clutching his shoe. Winston yelped and jumped back, where another hand through the grass grabbed at him. He kicked it and spun around. Hands were becoming arms, shoulders, and then heads as students pulled themselves up out of the ground. Their skin was rotted, their backpacks tattered.

"bbbi-i-igggo-o-ottt …" they moaned, rising to their feet. "bbbi-i-igggo-o-ottt …"

"What is wrong with this school?" Winston yelled. "Pod people *and* zombies?"

Winston swung around in a circle, his trumpet case at the ready. The zombie students had all risen from the ground and were closing in, teeth chomping, arms outstretched.

"What?" Winston said. "Do you want me to deny reality? Is that what students are expected to do here? Well, I won't! That's not a unicorn, okay? Maybe you all like to pretend it is, but it's not!"

"bbbi-i-igggo-o-ottt …" they moaned, coming closer. "bbbi-i-igggo-o-ottt …"

Winston swung his trumpet case, knocking the closest zombie student to the ground. The parking lot was a minute's run away.

"BIGOT!"

Winston winced as he heard the high shriek and saw a stream of students sprinting out one side of the school. Flattop led the way, along with the rest of the jocks.

"BIGOT!"

That came from the other side, two streams of shrieking students now angling toward Winston, the zombie students shuffling closer.

"That's it!" Winston said. "Screw marching band! I'm signing up for an online school!"

A hand grabbed his backpack, but he shrugged the bag off, throwing his trumpet case in the face of the closest student. He raced toward the parking lot, zigzagging through the students as he dodged grasping hands.

"BIGOT!" the sprinters shrieked.

"bbbi-i-igggo-o-ottt ..." the zombies moaned.

"BIGOT!"

"bbbi-i-igggo-o-ottt ..."

Winston ran as fast as he could, his lungs straining, the parking lot getting closer. Defiant, he yelled over his shoulder. "That's not a bleeping unicorn!"

Meanwhile, the donkey continued to enjoy its snack of green bushes outside Room E's window. They tasted so much better than the potted plants it was normally given. Then it noticed a flower on the ground between the bushes. Straining to reach it, the donkey pushed its body further through the window, but something on its head got caught within the bushes and something sticky pulled on its hair. The donkey shook its head in irritation and was relieved to feel the stickiness come loose and whatever had been on its head fall off. Content, it bent down and bit the flower from its stem.

You Never Had a Brother

WHAT'S WRONG, MOM? WHY ARE YOU CRYING? IT'S *my brother? What about my brother? What is he doing now? Please don't tell me he's gotten worse."*

▷ ◁

He remembered a beautiful, warm day, blue sky above and the sun shining down as he and his brother ran through the sprinklers in their front yard, shirts off, feet bare, wearing only swimsuits.

"I'm first to jump over the center one!" his brother said, raising both hands high while jumping and then pumping them low after landing on the wet grass.

"I'm first to jump over the broken one!" he said, mimicking his brother in both jump and landing.

"The broken one doesn't go as high."

He ignored this challenge from his brother and chased instead, the two of them zigzagging through the yard, the grass soft and slick under their feet. Fluffy clouds floated lazily across the sky. There was a soft, quiet breeze and birds chattered cheerfully in the tall trees above.

"Let's play the kidnapper game!" his brother said.

"Kidnappers in the rain!"

Their street was almost busy, almost busy for young boys at least. A car passed every minute or two. Now, whenever a car drove by, they stood straight, arms out, and pretended to be trees.

"They can't kidnap us if we're trees!" his brother had said when they first played the game months earlier.

But standing still can't hold the attention of young boys for long, and soon the two were running around the yard again.

"Watch this!" his brother said and then flopped down on top of a sprinkler, bare stomach blocking the water's flow.

"Uh uh uh uh uh uh uh," his brother said, letting the spraying water sound a rhythm.

"Watch this!" he said and then sat down atop a sprinkler, the water pushing up on his blue swimsuit. Water sprayed out underneath him, bouncing the fabric of his swimsuit where it hung below his legs.

They both laughed, and then they ran and they chased and they zigged and they zagged, the sun warm, the water cool, the grass wet, the two brothers.

They slid on the grass for a moment, challenging each other to slide further. But they quickly stopped after noticing the pulled-up grass. Their mom hated it when they did that. That didn't always stop them—they were young boys, after all—but today they were happy, and not sliding was a little thing, and maybe if they were good, just maybe, she'd let them have popsicles later.

A neighbor girl was walking past their yard with her dog. She was in second grade, older than he was but younger than his brother. And although he didn't understand why, when he saw her, he felt embarrassed. She was walking along the sidewalk, her black terrier pulling at the leash to come and sniff them. He should say "Hi." He should wave. But he sat on the grass instead, pulling his knees up and resting his head on them, eyes closed, the water from a sprinkler spraying onto his back.

"Hey!" his brother said to him, but he didn't move.

"Hey!" his brother repeated. Then he felt water hitting his head; and, looking up, he saw his brother in front of him, hands cupped over a sprinkler, diverting the blue stream right at him. His brother smiled. The neighbor girl was gone.

"Stop that!" he said, and then he got up and rushed at his brother, tackling him with a giggle, the two of them rolling around on the wet ground, blades of grass sticking to their bare torsos.

Then they were up and jumping again, higher, always higher, competing against each other, just like boys do.

"Watch this!" His brother jumped over the center sprinkler, kicking legs to the side and yelling.

"Watch this!" He followed after, spreading his legs as he jumped, the water striking the bottom of his swimsuit.

They laughed together. Then they ran and jumped and ran and jumped, his brother always able to jump higher, his brother always able to run faster; and the whole time he followed, he the little brother, his brother the hero.

➤ ◄

"No, we haven't spoken in months. He won't talk to me any-
more. He says I don't accept him. Accept him? I love him!
He's my brother! I want what's best for him! I can't just sit
back and see what he's doing and not say anything. But what
about his counselor? Didn't you encourage him to see one?
Isn't that helping?"

➤ ◄

He remembered being in the backyard with his brother,
the neighborhood outside their fence full of the whir of
lawn mowers and leaf blowers, the two brothers standing
side by side, both giggling as separate streams of pee arced
up and onto the bush behind their house.

"Mine is higher!" his brother said, pee almost reaching
a yellow sunflower that rocked lazily in the slight breeze.

Higher. That's how it always was between them. Higher.
Faster. Stronger. He thought of an earlier year. He thought
of two boys running bare-chested through the sprinklers.
Higher, always higher. He had to get higher. He had to
match his brother. Higher. But he was shorter, and he
hadn't drunk enough, and his stream was lower, already
starting to spurt out.

The warm yellow sun was high overhead. They had been
playing; they had been laughing; they had needed to pee,
and now they were. No reason for it. They both knew better. No reason for it at all. No reason beyond being stupid

boys. They would be skinned alive if they got caught. Of course, that was half the fun. And if his brother was doing it, he was going to, too.

"I'm gonna make it. I'm gonna make it," his brother said, yellow stream reaching higher, higher, and then—yes!—striking a leaf of the sunflower, which bobbed to the flow.

Higher, always higher. They both laughed.

"His counselor is encouraging it? What? That's malpractice! What if he thought he was Napoleon? Would his counselor encourage that too? I can't believe his counselor is encouraging it. It's not reality! He's not Napoleon. He's not anything else. He's my brother. My brother!"

He remembered sitting on the stairs as he looked through the railing, feeling green with jealousy as he watched his brother stand by the fireplace next to the neighbor girl, his brother in a prom tuxedo, the neighbor girl in a tight green dress. Of all the girls his brother could have asked, his brother had asked her.

He stared at the neighbor girl. He had had a crush on her for years. Maybe if he had told his brother about the crush, his brother wouldn't have asked her. But he hadn't told his brother, and now his brother stood there next to her, a boutonniere pinned to the tuxedo's jacket, the neighbor girl looking amazing, bare feet in the lush carpet, high heels in her hands, shiny jewels in her hair—not real jewels, but to him they shined like they were.

Higher, always higher. Two boys peeing in the bushes. Two boys jumping over sprinklers. Higher, always higher. Yes, someday he would be standing there too. Maybe not with the neighbor girl but with someone, someone just as pretty, someone who had said yes to his invitation, someone who would smile just as much, who would laugh at his jokes, just like the neighbor girl was laughing at his brother's jokes. Higher, always higher.

Sitting there on the stairs, he watched his brother. His brother seemed so happy, so excited. His mother was taking pictures on her cell phone. Nowadays, everyone saw each other's dresses before they even saw each other. His mother was wearing a dress too, not going anywhere but wearing a dress anyway, wearing a dress to take pictures, pictures that would be sent so everyone could see what they were wearing before they even saw them.

His father had put on a green tie and was standing there behind his mother, being corny. That's what fathers were for. His brother was laughing, an arm behind the neighbor girl's back. Everyone looked so happy. Everyone except for him.

➤　◀

"He's mixed up! Are they going to just leave him like that? What do they expect us to do, just go along with it? It's a lie! We can't pretend it's not a lie!"

▷   ◁

He remembered sitting in the stands at his brother's college graduation, the students a sea of black caps and gowns, his mother next to him. She held his hand tightly as they watched his brother walk down the aisle toward the stage, his brother looking so proud, multiple tassels tied to a black cap. He and his brother had grown distant after his brother left for college, an unsaid weight resting between the two of them. He didn't know what it was, but there was something his brother wasn't telling him. However, now wasn't a time for worries. Now was a time to celebrate his brother and his brother's accomplishment—because they were brothers. Higher, always higher. Soon it would be him walking down the aisle to collect his diploma. Higher, always higher. How did his brother get so many tassels? What did that mean? He'd have to find out. He couldn't have less when he graduated. Higher, always higher, like prom dates, like peeing on bushes, like jumping over sprinklers. Higher, always higher—because they were brothers.

It was crowded, the stands full of families there to celebrate the accomplishments of their loved ones. The rules called for quiet until the end, but you still had the occasional outburst from people who ignored the rules, rude noisemakers filling the air with their annoying blare. And sound wasn't the only thing filling the air. Someone nearby was wearing way too much perfume. Probably the old woman who sat in front of them, her dyed-black hair gigantic, rising in a beehive above her head.

"Now that's some Texas-sized hair," his mother had whispered after the woman sat down. It was so high his mother had to lean to one side in order to see the students below. But that was before and now was now and now they were watching his brother walk proudly forward to collect a diploma.

"I wish your father could be here," his mother said.

"I'm sure he's watching," he told her. "He'd want to be here for his son."

➤ ◄

"What? He can't do that! We can't let him do that! That's not some stupid tattoo. That's not some stupid body piercing. That's permanent mutilation! That's a mistake he can't take back. What? You've got to be joking. He's going to change his birth certificate too? How can he do that? It's a lie! We were there!"

➤ ◄

Blue was the sky as they ran through the sprinklers, bare-chested, laughing, jumping over this sprinkler, sliding under that one. They were playing follow the leader now. His brother had led him in circles around the sprinklers, both of them turning so much they became dizzy. Now it was his turn.

Tired of running, he sat down on a sprinkler, position-ing himself to completely block its spray.

"You sit on that one!" he told his brother, pointing to a sprinkler close to him.

His brother said nothing.

"Sit on that one!" he repeated, pointing again.

His brother still said nothing.

"It's my turn to be leader," he said, turning around to see why his brother was ignoring him.

But his brother wasn't there.

He leaped to his feet, confused. His brother had been right behind him a moment ago. Then he saw the hole in the ground where his brother had been, not a sinkhole, not a real hole, just a hole—a hole in reality itself, like a giant eraser had come down and rubbed his brother out of existence.

He looked at the hole, his eyes wide, his chest tight. This is wrong.

And a sprinkler next to the hole turned its head to face him, metal grooves bending, forming the crude outline of a pair of eyes and an empty mouth.

"What are you looking for?" the sprinkler asked. "There is nothing there."

"I'm looking for my brother."

"You never had a brother."

➤　◀

"Why is the world feeding into his delusion? Why are they encouraging it? Do they expect everyone to embrace the lie? We were there!"

⊳ ◄

Yellow were the streams as they peed on the bush behind their house. *I've got to reach the sunflower*, he told himself. If his brother could do it, then he had to do it too. He pushed harder; he raised himself higher; but he couldn't reach as high as his brother did.

And then his brother's stream was gone.

Confused, he looked to the side; but, where his brother had stood a moment before, there was a clear wall of nothing, a thin arc of nothing extending from the wall of nothing to strike the leaf of the sunflower, the sunflower still bobbing to a flow that wasn't there anymore.

He blinked his eyes, not believing what he was seeing. It was like someone had ripped a page, like someone had torn his brother out of reality itself.

Then the sunflower started to move, turning toward him. He watched as a crude pair of eyes formed within the flower's center, an empty mouth below them.

"What are you looking for?" the sunflower asked. "There is nothing there."

"I'm looking for my brother."

"You never had a brother. You never had a brother."

⊳ ◄

"They can't just pretend reality isn't reality. He is what he is. He was born what he is. We were there!"

Green was his envy as he watched the neighbor girl smile at his brother, the not-real-jewels sparkling in her hair, his mother taking pictures, his father being corny. He looked at his brother standing there with an arm around the neighbor girl's back. Why couldn't that be him?

Then there was a loud snap and a bright flash. He blinked his eyes and was shocked to see his brother's tuxedo standing there empty for a moment before crumpling slowly to the floor. Grasping the rails, he leaned forward for a better look. What had happened? No one else seemed to notice. The neighbor girl was chatting happily with the air beside her, his mother was still taking pictures. What would the pictures show?

Then the empty pants moved, a pant leg curling up, forming a crude pair of eyes above a wide empty mouth.

"What are you looking for?" the pants asked. "There is nothing there."

"I'm looking for my brother."

"You never had a brother. You never had a brother. You never had a brother."

▷   ◁

"You've got to talk him out of it somehow. Won't he listen to you? You're his mother. He has to listen to you. He won't listen to me, but he has to listen to you. This is a mistake. It's a mistake he can never take back. Talk to him. Talk him out of it. Talk him into waiting at least. Maybe we can find him a different counselor, a real counselor, a counselor that will encourage reality instead of make-believe. We have

to talk him out of it. This is a mistake he can never take back!"

> � ◄

Black were the caps and gowns as he watched his brother walk down the aisle toward the stage. His mother sat beside him; his father long gone. Someday it would be him walking down that aisle. He counted up the years before that date as he watched his brother draw closer to the stage. Soon his brother would be shaking the hand of the college president. A formality, but that meant college was officially over. His brother walked so confidently, so proudly.

Then his brother was gone.

He leaned forward. Where was his brother? Where was the aisle? The crowd of students sat shoulder to shoulder where his brother had been. The aisle itself had vanished. Except, it hadn't. In front and behind where his brother had been, the aisle was still there, and other students continued their march toward the stage. But where his brother had been, students sat instead. And the non-aisle moved, keeping the same pace his brother had kept, the aisle collapsing and then reopening, seated students becoming shoulder to shoulder before jumping apart again.

Then, in the row in front of him, the woman's large beehive hair began to move, the strands shifting their place, forming a crude pair of eyes above an empty mouth.

"What are you looking for?" the hair asked. "There is nothing there."

"I'm looking for my brother."

"You never had a brother. You never had a brother. You never had a brother. You never had a brother."

▷   ◁

"We have to stop him somehow. We have to talk him out of it. We can't let him do this to himself. I have a brother; no matter what he does. I have a brother; no surgery can change that. I have a brother; no fraudulent birth certificate can steal that away from me. I have a brother, not just a sibling, a brother! I have a brother!"

The Sky Is Blue

JOHNNY-BOY NEVER LEARNED A COLOR until he was five. That was when his mother drove him up the hill to the edge of the city. Then she took his small hand in her soft hand and led him up the mountain.

The air was crisp, the sun was warm, and the sky was beautiful. Johnny-boy didn't know what color the sky was—he hadn't been taught his colors yet—but whatever color it was, the sky was full of it, clear from the left to the right, from the top to the bottom, not a cloud in sight, only the bright sun floating high in the middle. Johnny-boy didn't know what color the sun was either, but he knew it must be something warm because of how toasty it felt on his cheeks, and his arms, and his stubby little legs below his shorts.

Johnny-boy and his mother walked, and they walked, and they walked, and they walked, until finally they came to the top of a hill. The hill was covered with grass, soft and wavy and moving in the breeze. And, looking down the other side of the hill, Johnny-boy could see a large lake that stretched on for what seemed like forever.

Then Johnny-boy's mother took his two small hands in her two soft hands and smiled down at him. "You're such a big boy, Johnny-boy," she told him. "You're such a big boy that now it's time for you to learn your colors. Are you ready to learn your colors, Johnny-boy?"

Johnny-boy smiled up at his mother. "Yes, Mommy," he said. "Please teach me my colors." He was so excited he wanted to skip around, but he stood patiently instead because Mommy liked it when he was patient and still.

She patted his head, the smile still on her face. Then she pointed at the ground. "Do you see the grass, Johnny-boy?" she asked.

"Yes, Mommy, it's all over the hill. It's so soft and so squishy; I just want to roll around in it!"

"That's good, Johnny-boy," she said. "Now look at the grass. The grass is green. Can you say that, Johnny-boy? What color is the grass?"

"It's green, Mommy!" he said, staring at the grass—the green grass—with delight.

"That's right!" his mother said. She clasped his two small hands and shook them up and down excitedly. Then she stood up again and pointed down the other side of the hill. "Now look at the lake, Johnny-boy. Do you see the water below?"

"Yes, Mommy!" Johnny-boy said. "It goes on forever and forever, and it looks so cool. I wish I could jump in it right now!"

"That's good, Johnny-boy," she said. "Now look at the lake. The lake is blue. Can you say that, Johnny-boy? What color is the lake?"

"It's blue, Mommy!"

"That's right!" his mother said, once again bending over to shake his two small hands up and down. "Oh,

Johnny-boy, my precious little Johnny-boy, you are so smart, and you are such a good, good boy."

Then she straightened up and stared at him for a moment. "Now, I'm going to ask you one more question, Johnny-boy," she told him, "and I'm sure such a smart, good boy like yourself will get that question right. Will you answer my question right, Johnny-boy?"

"Yes, Mommy!" he said, eager to please her, and he waited for her question.

But she didn't ask it. She just stood there for a moment longer and stared at him, the smile frozen on her face. And suddenly Johnny-boy noticed movement all around him. The grass was standing up.

No, the grass wasn't standing up—people were standing up from the grass. See-through people. He could see their outlines; he could see their shadows; but they were clear, completely see-through, like there was nothing there.

"Look at me, Johnny-boy," his mother commanded. Her two soft hands yanked on his two small hands.

Johnny-boy's head jerked back toward his mother. "But, Mommy," he said, his voice shaking. "Who are these people? Why are they see-through?"

Then the see-through people began to move, their vague outlines twisting and contorting as they spun around Johnny-boy and his mother, the see-through people chanting together:

The sky is green. The sky is green. The sky is green. The sky is green.

Once again, his mother's soft hands yanked his attention back to her. "Look at me, Johnny-boy!" she commanded.

The sky is green. The sky is green. The sky is green. The sky is green.

"But, Mommy!" he wailed, watching the see-through people twist and turn as they spun around and chanted.

The sky is green. The sky is green. The sky is green. The sky is green.

"Look at me, Johnny-boy!" his mother commanded again.

And Johnny-boy obeyed. He stared up at her eyes, trying as hard as he could not to notice the see-through people twisting all around them.

The sky is green. The sky is green. The sky is green. The sky is green.

"Johnny-boy," his mother said, her voice almost menacing. "Look up at the sky, Johnny-boy. What color is the sky? What color is the sky, my smart, good, little Johnny-boy?"

The sky is green. The sky is green. The sky is green. The sky is green.

All around him the see-through people twisted as they turned and they chanted.

The sky is green. The sky is green. The sky is green. The sky is green.

Johnny-boy looked up at the sky. His mother hadn't told him what color it was yet. He looked down at the grass. The grass was green. Then Johnny-boy looked out at the lake. The lake was blue. Johnny-boy looked up at the sky again.

The sky is green. The sky is green. The sky is green. The sky is green.

"Johnny-boy," his mother said. Her grip was hurting his hands. "What color is the sky, Johnny-boy?"

The sky is green. The sky is green. The sky is green. The sky is green.

Johnny-boy looked down at the grass. The grass was green. He looked out at the lake. The lake was blue. He looked up at the sky. It looked like the lake.

"It's blue, Mommy," he said. "The sky is blue."

She slapped him across the face.

The sky is green. The sky is green. The sky is green. The sky is green.

Johnny-boy started to cry. He could still feel her finger marks on his cheek. Mommy had never hit him before. What had he done wrong? He wanted to ask her, but she had turned her back on him.

The sky is green. The sky is green. The sky is green. The sky is green.

The see-through people twisted, and the see-through people chanted, and Johnny-boy's mother just stood there, her back toward him, looking away. Johnny-boy cried. His cheek stung.

Then, a moment later, his mother turned back to him. "Johnny-boy," she said. "What color is the sky?"

The sky is green. The sky is green. The sky is green. The sky is green.

The see-through people were all around him, but Johnny-boy tried not to look at them. Mommy didn't like it when he noticed the see-through people.

"What color is the sky, Johnny-boy?" she asked again.

Johnny-boy looked down at the grass. The grass was green. He looked out at the lake. The lake was blue. He looked up at the sky. The sky looked like the lake.

"It's blue, Mommy," he repeated.

She slapped him again, striking him so hard she knocked him off his stubby little legs.

The sky is green. The sky is green. The sky is green. The sky is green.

Johnny-boy lay there on the ground, sobbing into the green grass. He looked up at his mother, but she had her back turned to him again. The see-through people were still twisting, contorting, and chanting.

The sky is green. The sky is green. The sky is green. The sky is green.

What had he done wrong? Hadn't he answered her question? She had taught him what color grass was, and she had taught him what color the lake was, and the sky looked like the lake. What had he done wrong?

Then his mother turned around again. Reaching down, she grabbed one of his small hands with one of her soft hands and lifted him back onto his stubby little legs. Then, looking down at him, she asked in a quiet voice: "Johnny-boy, what color is the sky?"

The sky is green. The sky is green. The sky is green. The sky is green.

Johnny-boy looked down at the grass. The grass was green. He looked out at the lake. The lake was blue. The sky looked like the lake.

The sky is green. The sky is green. The sky is green. The sky is green.

"Johnny-boy," his mother repeated, her voice so soft he could barely hear it. "What color is the sky, Johnny-boy?"

Johnny-boy stared up into his mother's eyes. "Green?"

"Oh, Johnny-boy!" His mother bent down and embraced him. "My smart little Johnny-boy! You are such a good boy! I'm so proud of you!" She held him for a moment before letting go. "Now, tell me one more time, will you Johnny-boy? Tell me one more time so Mommy will know that her smart little Johnny-boy knows his colors. What color is the sky, Johnny-boy?"

Johnny-boy's cheek still stung from her slaps. "It's green, Mommy. The sky is green."

"Oh, such a good boy," she said, and she gave him another hug.

The sky is green. The sky is green. The sky is green. The sky is green.

His mother stood up and took his small hand in her soft hand. The see-through people kept moving, chanting, twisting; but they made way for Johnny-boy's mother to lead him back down the hill.

The sky is green. The sky is green. The sky is green. The sky is green.

"You're such a good little boy, Johnny-boy," his mother said, smiling at him as they walked down the hill. "Do you like being such a good little boy?"

"Yes, Mommy," Johnny-boy said. "I like being a good little boy." And he smiled back up at her. Except his smile was a lie. Inside, he was screaming: "It's blue, Mommy! It's blue! The sky is blue! Why won't you let me tell you the truth that it's blue?"

Stare Decisis

A man sat down on his couch and picked up his remote. "Honey, it's almost time for the game to start," he called into the other room. Then he turned on the TV, and the title of a show appeared: *Constitutional Law 101.*

An announcer walked on to the screen in front of a background of puzzled faces. "Have you been confused by recent events?" the announcer asked. "When you heard that judges had declared that the Constitution required same-sex marriage, did you wonder what was being passed around in those judges' chambers?"

A dark, smoke-filled room appeared on the screen, multiple people in black robes sitting around a small wooden table. A glass bong was seen briefly as it was passed from one person to the next. Somewhere in the room, someone was giggling.

Then the announcer was back in front of the wall of confused faces. "Have you stared and stared at the Constitution, wondering how in the world a judge could find a requirement for same-sex marriage inside those words?"

The scene shifted to a young man sitting at a desk, his wife standing behind him and looking over his shoulder.

"I've read it again and again!" the young man said, shaking his head in bewilderment. "But I don't see anything about same-sex marriage in the Constitution!"

"Did you check the penumbras?" his equally confused wife asked. "What about the penumbras of the penumbras?"

On the couch, watching the TV, the man scratched his chin. "Honey, what's a penumbra?"

"It's like a region in partial shadow, dear," a woman called from the other room.

"No, this is something to do with the law."

"Oh, *that* kind of penumbra. That's just a BS excuse used by judges when they're pulling a ruling out of their—"

"The Constitution!" The announcer was walking across the screen, a giant Constitution behind him. Patriotic music began to play.

"We wrote the Constitution because we wanted to protect our liberties," the announcer said. "We wanted freedom of speech. We wanted freedom of religion. We wanted freedom to not have troops quartered in our homes."

An old couple appeared on the screen, standing in their front yard. The old man put his arm around his wife's shoulders.

"There will be no troops quartered in *our* home!" the old man said.

The old woman nodded. "Thank you, Constitution!"

"That's right," the announcer said, appearing on the screen in front of the giant Constitution again. "The Constitution was written to protect those rights and more. But what has happened to it? How is it that judges are able to twist it into such strange shapes? That's what we're here to talk about today."

The front door of a house appeared, the house a crisp shade of blue, the door a spotless white. The door opened, showing a happy, smiling family standing in the doorway: a young girl in pigtails, a mother wearing a red apron, and a father sporting a manly mustache.

"This family wants a cute, fluffy kitten," the announcer said.

There was a flash and suddenly the little girl was holding a cute, fluffy kitten.

"I love my cute, fluffy kitty!" the little girl said, rubbing the kitten's fur against her cheek.

"Meow?" the kitten said.

The announcer appeared once more, standing in front of the giant Constitution. "We wanted a Constitution that protected our basic liberties, but we can't think of everything when we write our laws."

The scene switched to the family again. They were standing in their house at the bottom of the stairs.

"Oh, no!" the mother exclaimed as they watched the kitten struggle to climb onto the bottom stair. "We forgot about our tall stairs!"

The little girl turned to face the audience. "We wanted a cute, fluffy kitty, but our cute, fluffy kitty can't climb our stairs!"

"Never fear, little girl!" the announcer said. "That's what judges are for! You didn't think of those tall stairs when you wanted your cute, fluffy kitten, but judges can look at the intent of our laws and fit them to unexpected circumstances. Why, here's a judge right now."

There was a flash and suddenly a judge in black robes was standing next to the family.

"Oh, Mr. Judge, Mr. Judge," the little girl said, grabbing hold of his hand. "Please help our cute, fluffy kitty, Mr. Judge!"

"Of course, little girl," the judge said, patting her on the head. Then he pulled a small black bag out of his robe.

"See that, audience?" the announcer said, his voice a low whisper. "Every judge is entrusted with a bag of judicial ruling dust. Let's watch what happens."

The judge sprinkled some of the magical dust onto the kitten.

"Meow?"

Suddenly four furry appendages burst out of the kitten's back; like giant spider legs, they arched up and then down onto the floor.

"Oh!" the mother said, grabbing her husband's arm. "I didn't expect that to happen!"

The kitten reached two furry spider legs up onto the bottom stair. Lifting itself up, it climbed onto the stair, then the next. Then it climbed back down. Then back up.

The father clapped in excitement. "Now it can climb the stairs!"

"Yes, but are you sure those are necessary?" the mother asked, pointing at the furry spider legs growing out of the kitten's back.

The little girl picked up the kitten. "I love my cute, fluffy kitty," the little girl said, holding it to her check. It reached one of its furry spider legs around and stoked the little girl's other cheek. "It's a little bit freaky," the little girl said, pushing the furry spider leg away from her face, "but I still love it!"

"Don't you see, audience?" the announcer said, suddenly in the room with the family. "Thanks to the judge's magical dust, the kitten can now walk up and down the stairs. The judicial ruling dust created a precedent, and that precedent isn't likely to go away."

"Are you sure?" the mother asked. "Because I was thinking maybe we should move into a one-story house and then that precedent wouldn't be needed anymore."

"Oh, no," the announcer said, laughing as he put his hand on the mother's shoulder. "Now that a judge has gotten involved, your kitten is going to have freaky spider legs growing out of its back forever."

"Do you want to pet it, Mommy?" the little girl asked, holding out the kitten.

Four furry spider legs reached for the mother. "Meow?"

The mother hid behind her husband, who looked a little nervous despite his manly mustache.

"Yes," the announcer said, "precedent is just like furry spider legs growing out the back of your kitten that never go away. Sometimes useful. Sometimes a little bit freaky."

"I think that's more than a little bit freaky," the mother said, poking her head above her husband's shoulder. "Don't you think if we got a one-story house—"

"But sometimes," the announcer went on, "sometimes, our judges go sour. Power can do that to a person. Sometimes they forget their role, and sometimes they decide to take a more activist stance."

The judge pulled a crown out of his robe and put it atop his head. He tossed his black bag of judicial ruling dust onto the ground and pulled out a red bag labeled "Judicial Activism Dust." Then the newly crowned judge sprinkled some judicial activism dust on the kitten, and the four furry spider legs immediately shed their hair, the spider legs becoming tentacles, a tiny mouth forming on each tip.

"Aaaahh!" the little girl screamed, dropping the kitten to the floor.

"Meow?" The kitten stumbled toward the little girl, four tentacles on its back snapping their mouths as they strained to reach her.

"Aaaahh!" The little girl jumped behind her father. "What did the king judge do to my cute, fluffy kitty?"

"It's not such a cute, fluffy kitten anymore, is it?" the announcer said, shaking his head. "But what's worse, the activist rulings create precedents which spawn further activist rulings which create even worse precedents."

The king judge sprinkled more judicial activism dust on the kitten, and its tentacles grew and grew. He sprinkled more dust, and four additional tentacles burst out of the kitten's back.

"Meow?"

Eight mouths snarled at the family, tentacles twisting toward them.

"Aaaahh!" The family scattered in all directions.

The king judge skipped around the room, throwing judicial activism dust into the air. "I decree this! I decree that! I decree this! I decree that!"

And each time the magical dust hit the kitten or its tentacles, the tentacles grew thicker, longer, the mouths larger, now the size of a fist.

One of the mouths caught hold of the little girl's pigtail.

"Mommy!" the little girl cried as the mouth yanked on her hair.

"You let go of her!" the mother said, swatting at the tentacle with her apron. Letting go of the pigtail, the tentacle mouth twisted toward the mother instead. She screamed, and tried to shoo it away with her apron, but its teeth kept snapping at her.

Then the father was there. He pushed his wife and daughter behind him. "Leave my family alone, you ugly, activism-inspired tentacle mouth!"

The mouth darted forward and seized hold of his mustache. It jerked backward, ripping half of the mustache away.

"Ow!" the father yelled, a hand to his face. "It ripped off my manly mustache!"

The announcer appeared on the screen again. "That's right, audience," the announcer said. "Judicial activism hates manly mustaches."

Tentacles twisted this way and that, mouths snapping at the family, who kept running around the room, trying to escape. But there were too many tentacles, and too many mouths. The family couldn't get away.

"You see, audience," the announcer said. "Activist rulings beget activist rulings, and the precedent piles higher and higher until the law bears no resemblance to the law we created in the first place. Just look at this cute, fluffy kitten."

The camera zoomed in on the kitten's cute, fluffy face.

"Meow?" the kitten said.

The family stopped running. "Aww," they said together as they smiled at the kitten.

"I love my cute, fluffy kitty!" the little girl said.

Then the camera zoomed back out, showing the eight giant tentacles growing out of the kitten's back, their eight mouths growling at the family as they hovered in the air.

"Aaaahh!" the family screamed and started running again. The tentacle mouths twisted after them.

"We wanted a constitution to protect our basic liberties," the announcer said, "just like this family wanted a cute, fluffy kitten. But look at what judicial activism has transformed it into: a mutated monster of mayhem."

A tentacle mouth sunk its teeth into the mother's finger. She screamed, shaking her hand desperately, but the mouth wouldn't let go. Then the scene zoomed in for a close-up of the announcer's face.

"Now do you understand how judges find a right for same-sex marriage in the Constitution?"

A tentacle twisted past his face, a severed finger hanging out of its mouth. Then the scene zoomed back out to show the whole room again, tentacles twisting in every direction as they chased after the frantic family.

"And what can we do about it?" the announcer asked, shaking his head at the scene. "Are we stuck with this mess forever?" He spread out his arms, gesturing at the madness all around.

"Well, I have a solution!" he said. "And here's step one!" The announcer grabbed the king judge by the scruff of the neck, halting him mid-skip.

"I declare—oh!"

The announcer swatted the crown and bag of judicial activism dust onto the ground. Then he dragged the king judge toward the front door.

"You can't do this!" the king judge protested, struggling against the announcer's grip. "You can't do this! I have life tenure! You're supposed to be stuck with my nonsense for decades!"

But the announcer paid him no mind. He opened the door and then, giving the king judge a much-deserved kick in the rear, sent him flying out of the house.

"Now for step two," the announcer said as he turned back inside. There was a flash and suddenly he held a machete in his hand. Grabbing a tentacle below its mouth, he raised his machete high. The mouth turned toward him, hissing and baring its teeth, but the announcer shouted in response and struck with his machete—

The man on the couch changed the channel. A woman appeared on the screen, standing in a kitchen. She set a large bowl of salad down onto the counter.

"And that's how you make a tossed salad!"

The man on the couch changed the channel again. A goat's face appeared, the goat staring straight at the screen, slowly chewing a mouth full of rubbish.

"Honey," the man on the couch called into the other room, "do you know what channel the game is on?"

The Statue of Liberty Orders a Burger

(and gets something completely different)

THE STATUE OF LIBERTY WALKED INTO HER favorite fast food restaurant, metal feet clanking on the tile as she strode up to the counter.

"Can I help you?" the politician, a middle-aged man in suit and tie, asked from behind the counter.

"Yes," the Statue of Liberty replied. "I'd like a burger and a shake."

"A burger and a shake?"

"Yes, a burger and a shake."

"Okay." The politician took out a piece of paper and wrote down the order: "A burger and a shake."

"We'll have that right out for you," he said. Then he turned around and handed the order to a judge in black robes who was standing behind him. The judge scribbled something on the order before handing it to another black-robed judge, who scribbled on it and then handed it to another, who repeated the process before handing it to the final black-robed judge, who read through the order and then walked back into the kitchen.

A moment later the judge returned, carrying a tray with a steaming pile of cow manure and a cup full of urine. He set it down on the counter in front of the Statue of Liberty, banged his gavel on the counter, and declared, "Your order is ready!"

"Are you mental?" the Statue of Liberty asked. "That's a pile of cow manure and a cup of urine! I ordered a burger and a shake!"

"Yes, that's what you ordered *originally*," the judge said, "But then the first judge made her ruling and set a precedent, and then the second judge made his ruling and set another precedent, and then the third judge made her ruling and set yet another precedent, and it was only then that I got the order to consider."

"Yes, an order for a burger and a shake!"

"Right, that was your *original* order; but after I took all the established precedents into account, they led to an inevitable ruling: a pile of cow manure and a cup of urine."

"No!" the Statue of Liberty shouted, her righteous fury filling the restaurant. She shoved the tray back at the judge, manure and urine splattering on his robes as the tray hit him in the gut. Then the Statue of Liberty reached out a copper hand and seized the politician by the collar. She yanked him off his feet, pulling him right up to her face.

"Fire them!" the Statue of Liberty commanded, pointing her torch at the judges cowering behind the counter. "Fire them all! Hire someone competent enough to understand that a burger is a bleeping burger!"

The Honor Code on Trial

JEFFREY DIDN'T HAVE TIME FOR THIS. HE had to be at the airport in two hours, and if he missed his flight, he'd miss classes tomorrow. But here he was, walking into the offices of the Northeast Accreditation Commission in Boston, delivering a message that could have just as easily been delivered over the phone.

"I don't get why you want me to tell them," Jeffrey had told his friend Scott on the phone that morning.

"Because you're the perfect messenger for this," Scott had said.

"That makes no sense. I'm a computer guy. I don't do politics or logistics or nonsense like that. You work in the admin office. Get someone from there."

"No, you're perfect for it," Scott said. "You're blunt. They need to hear blunt."

"What is this even about?" Jeffrey asked.

"Oh, you'll see. I only wish you could videotape it."

"What exactly are you getting me into?"

"Don't worry about it. You'll do fine. I'm telling you, you're the perfect messenger for this."

"Okay, but you're paying for dinner when I take your sister on that double date. And I'm not talking about fast food, either. I'm talking about a nice steak house. It's going to be a big bill, a really big bill."

And that was why Jeffrey had agreed to this annoying errand. He had been bribed. He would deliver this little message to the accreditation commission and then he would get to go out with Scott's sister. A fair trade, Jeffrey had decided, so long as this stupid meeting didn't make him miss his flight. He did wonder, though, about Scott's comment. Why would Scott want to videotape it, and why did Scott think Jeffrey was the perfect messenger? What was Scott expecting him to do exactly? Sure, Jeffrey might drop his filter at times and be a little too blunt, but he would be representing BYU here. He couldn't say or do something inappropriate or something that would reflect poorly on the school. What was Scott expecting?

Pushing open the door, Jeffrey walked inside the conference room. There was a large table in the middle of the room, three people seated on the opposite side, one man and two women. None of them rose as he entered the room and no one offered to shake his hand.

"Take a seat," the man said, gesturing to the single chair on Jeffrey's side of the table. The man had a wide, friendly face and was wearing a large sweater, its pattern enhanced by the rolls down his sides.

"Okay," Jeffrey said as he sat down. "But I have to make this quick."

"Will anyone else be joining you?" the woman sitting on the left asked. She too wore a sweater, but hers was trim and pink. Jeffrey thought she probably had a lot of cats.

He was about to ask her how many she had, but then he reminded himself he was representing BYU and needed to behave.

"No, just me," he said. "Listen, I have a flight to catch, but here is what I was asked to tell you—"

"Hold on just a moment," the pink-sweatered woman said. "Let's get some introductions first. My name is Professor Carroll, and this is Professor Walsh," she said, pointing to the large man who sat between her and the other woman.

"Hello!" Professor Walsh said, and he offered the most natural grin Jeffrey had ever seen.

"And that's Ms. Hursh," Professor Carroll continued as she pointed to the woman sitting on the right. Small and slender, Ms. Hursh had the prettiest face in the room, yet it somehow made Jeffrey think of long-term food storage, dried-up and tasteless. He didn't think she had any cats. Reptiles seemed more likely, but Jeffrey kept that opinion to himself. He was representing his school, after all.

"Great, well, I'm Jeffrey Bruder. I'm a graduate student at BYU and I was asked to deliver a message on their behalf. I'm in a bit of a rush so I'll just say—"

"Wait … what?" Ms. Hursh said, leaning forward across the table. "BYU sent a *graduate student* to represent them?"

"That's highly irregular," Professor Walsh said, his grin gone, replaced by a look of confused concern.

"Yes, this is quite unexpected," Professor Carroll said. "Given the potentially serious consequences of this discussion, we expected that someone from BYU's administration would be attending."

"How predictable," Ms. Hursh said. She folded her arms, every angle of her body looking like it could draw blood. "They aren't even taking our concerns seriously."

"Please don't take this personally," Professor Carroll said, "but why did they send you?"

Jeffrey shrugged. "Apparently I'm the perfect messenger."

Professor Walsh turned to Professor Carroll. "Can we even proceed? Are we allowed to?"

"I think we have to."

Jeffrey put his hands on his knees. "I just have a short message to give."

"How predictable that their perfect messenger would be male," Ms. Hursh said, glaring at Jeffrey. Definitely too cold-blooded for cats, he thought.

Professor Carroll and Professor Walsh were whispering back and forth. Then Professor Carroll patted Professor Walsh on his arm and nodded in Jeffrey's direction.

"Mr. Jeffrey," Professor Walsh began.

"Bruder," Professor Carroll corrected him. "It's Mr. Bruder."

"Jeffrey is fine," Jeffrey told them, anxious to move the conversation along.

"Oh, my! Thank you," Professor Walsh said. "Now, Jeffrey, you said you were the perfect messenger, yes?"

Jeffrey shrugged. "Sure, and I was just asked to say—"

Professor Carroll held up a hand. "Please let Professor Walsh continue."

Jeffrey leaned back in his chair and glanced at his watch, his foot starting to tap on the ground impatiently. If this meeting makes me miss my flight. . . .

Professor Walsh cleared his throat. "Thank you, Professor Carroll. Now, Jeffrey, as we mentioned in our letter, the reason we summoned you here today is to talk about your school's honor code."

"Okay," Jeffrey said. Lots of people complained about BYU's honor code. Of course, that was the nice thing about having so many universities to choose from. If you didn't like the standards of one university, you were free to go somewhere else.

Professor Walsh went on. "We are concerned that your honor code violates our non-discrimination policy."

Jeffrey wasn't sure if he'd heard Professor Walsh correctly. "Our honor code violates your what?"

"Our non-discrimination policy," Professor Walsh said. "Our policy against discrimination. We're concerned, Jeffrey. It is imperative that a university not discriminate against any of its students."

Jeffrey thought through the rules of the honor code, but sitting there in front of these three members of the accreditation commission, he couldn't think of anything that would justify that concern. "I don't get it," he said. "We don't ban anyone from attending so long as they agree to abide by the honor code."

Then Jeffrey got a little mischievous. "I guess you do need pretty good grades and test scores to get in though," he said. "That's not really because of the honor code, but is that what you're getting at? You're worried that we discriminate against people who don't get good grades?"

"Oh, my!" Professor Walsh said. "I never thought of that before. That is discrimination, isn't it? Oh, my! That's something to think about." He turned to Professor Carroll. "Should we ban colleges from having grade- and test-based admittance criteria?"

Professor Carroll shook her head. "No, no, no. That's not what we're talking about at all."

"Then what are you getting at?" Jeffrey asked, reminding himself that now wasn't the time for poking fun. "We don't ban anyone. If you want to attend, then you abide by the standards in the honor code. It's as simple as that."

Ms. Hursh scoffed at his answer, her arms seeming to fold even further into herself, but it was Professor Carroll that responded. "But that's just it, Jeffrey," she said. "You say that it's simple, but that's only because you are looking at it from a privileged viewpoint. What you fail to realize, what BYU fails to realize, is that your honor code restricts some students from being themselves, and to restrict a student from being herself is just as bad as banning her. It's discrimination, Jeffrey. It needs to stop."

Jeffrey had no idea what they were talking about. *Scott is probably back in Utah laughing right now*, he thought. *Perfect messenger? Why did he think I was the perfect messenger? I don't even understand what they're saying! Privileged viewpoint? What am I supposed to say to this nonsense?*

But he had to say something. "How," he began, straining to be respectful. Then he adjusted his question. "Who—"

The door behind him burst open and a woman walked in, carrying a paper drink carrier with three steaming coffee cups.

"Our coffee!" Professor Walsh cheered.

The woman placed a coffee cup in front of each of the three at the table. Then she turned to Jeffrey. "I'm so sorry," she said, "Did you want some coffee? I didn't realize there was going to be four of you. When I heard that Professor Murray would be gone, I thought it would only be three."

"Oh, no," Jeffrey said, smiling at the woman, who was actually quite pretty. "I'm alright."

She smiled in return, causing Jeffrey to forget his annoyance for a moment. Then she left the room.

"Oh, my! That's good coffee!" Professor Walsh said after his first sip.

"It certainly is," Professor Carroll agreed.

"I've never had coffee from this shop before," Ms. Hursh said, scowling at the logo on her cup before taking a drink. "Is it organic?"

"Oh, my! Definitely!" Professor Walsh said.

"And their workers, are they paid a living wage?"

"Oh, my! Yes!" Professor Walsh said. "It's a very progressive corporation."

Ms. Hursh sniffed. "They all claim that." She stuck her nose to the opening and took a brief sniff. "But what about the beans?" she asked suspiciously. "Are they fair trade?"

"Yes, yes, yes," Professor Carroll said, waving her hand to ward off further questions. "Take a drink. It's wonderful."

Ms. Hursh grunted, but she put the cup to her lips and took a small drink. Then she nodded. "It's acceptable," she said.

"This is the best cup of coffee I've ever had!" Professor Walsh said. He tilted his cup up higher and took another drink. "Oh, my! I burned my tongue!" He laughed. Then he looked over at Jeffrey. "Are you sure you don't want any? I'm telling you, the best coffee I've ever had!"

"No, thanks. I don't drink coffee."

"You don't drink coffee?" Ms. Hursh said. "Why would someone not drink coffee?"

"I'm Mormon," Jeffrey said. "Mormons don't drink coffee."

"Why not?" Professor Walsh asked with the honest curiosity of a grade-schooler.

Jeffrey shrugged. "It's a religious dietary code."

"How bizarre," Ms. Hursh said. She took another sip of her coffee but then suddenly stopped, panic filling her eyes. "Wait," she said and turned to her colleagues. "Is this coffee non-GMO?"

"Yes!" Professor Carroll said. "Yes, yes, yes! All the check boxes. Every one." And she waved her hand in the air as if she were holding a pencil and marking a check box.

"Well, that's a relief," Ms. Hursh said. "I was afraid I'd have to purge myself."

Jeffrey glanced at his watch again.

"Are you positive you don't want some?" Ms. Hursh asked Jeffrey, giving him a condescending look. "We won't tell on you, I promise."

"I'm sure," Jeffrey said.

"Your loss," she replied. "You church-goers and your religious dogma. I don't know how you enjoy anything in life." Then she took another sip of her organic, living-wage, fair-trade, non-GMO coffee.

Jeffrey put his hands back on his knees. "Well, how about I deliver my message and let you three enjoy your coffee. I gotta say, I really don't understand what you meant about us restricting people from being themselves, but as the message I was asked to deliver should make clear..."

Then Jeffrey paused, his attention caught by Professor Carroll, whose face was bright red, her lips pulled tightly together. "Uh, what is she doing?" he asked.

Professor Walsh glanced over. "Oh, she's just holding her breath. Go on ... go on ... she'll be done in another thirty seconds or so."

But there was no way Jeffrey was going to leave it at that. "Why in the world is she holding her breath?"

"She has to hold in some of her carbon dioxide to make up for the carbon footprint of her coffee," Professor Walsh said, as if it were the most natural thing in the world. "Breathing produces carbon dioxide; carbon dioxide is a greenhouse gas; greenhouse gases cause climate change; and climate change will cause the apocalypse if we don't stop it; so Professor Carroll, quite rightly, strives to be as carbon neutral as possible."

He turned to Professor Carroll, who was staring at her watch, her face bright red. "Speaking of which," he said, "I don't quite remember how much penance I must pay for my coffee, and I seem to have left my book of dogma and my scale at home. Would you be willing to weigh it out for me?"

Professor Carroll held up a finger, asking for more time as she continued to stare at her watch. Then she opened her mouth with a gasp.

"Professor Walsh explained it well," she said to Jeffrey after a moment of huffing and puffing. "It's all very scientific!"

She reached down and lifted her bag up onto the table. Then she pulled a well-worn leather book and an old two-sided scale out of the bag and placed them in front of her on the table.

The book was interesting (you don't see leather books very often anymore, other than scriptures), but it was the scale that caught Jeffrey's eye. Made of metal, it had a woman engraved in its center. But this wasn't blindfolded Lady Justice like you might expect. No, this woman had her eyes wide open and a finger pointed in a manner that can only be described as accusatory. She also had the most scolding expression on her face Jeffrey had ever seen. He would hate to meet her in real life.

Professor Carroll opened the book and flipped through the pages. "Let's see," she said. "Coffee … coffee … coffee … ah, here it is." She studied the page for a moment. Then she pulled a few small weights from her bag and placed them on the scale.

"Hmm," Professor Carroll said. "Looks like two minutes."

"You're going to hold your breath for two minutes because you enjoyed a cup of coffee?" Jeffrey asked. *And people think I'm missing out because I don't drink the stuff?*

"Oh, my!" Professor Walsh said, looking disturbed. "Jeffrey is absolutely right. You forgot to add my enjoyment penance!"

"There's an enjoyment penance too?" *Now Jeffrey was really glad he didn't drink coffee.*

"Oh, my! Yes!" Professor Walsh said. "Because the more I enjoy it, the more likely I am to do it again."

"It's all very scientific!" Professor Carroll said. Then, after she tinkered with the scale in an arcane fashion, she told Professor Walsh, "Two and a half minutes."

"Thank you," Professor Walsh said. "I'll perform my penance as soon as I finish my coffee."

"Then that will be extra," Ms. Hursh said.

"Why?" Jeffrey asked, unable to contain his curiosity at their ritual.

"Because it will still be hot," Ms. Hursh replied. "Better make it three minutes," she told Professor Walsh.

Wow, Jeffrey thought. What kind of craziness is in that coffee? "On that note," he said, starting to rise. "Let me just say what I was sent here—"

"Oh, no you don't!" Ms. Hursh cut him off.

Jeffrey sat back down. "What?" he asked. Ms. Hursh had seemed cold before. But it felt like she had just slapped him in the face.

"Check your privilege," Ms. Hursh said. "I don't know what it's like at BYU, but with us your Y chromosome doesn't make you entitled to speak first."

"But I have a flight to catch," Jeffrey said, looking again at his watch. "Can't we at least make this quick?"

Professor Carroll shut her book. "Jeffrey, I don't think you're taking the situation as seriously as it warrants."

You just held your breath because you're afraid your carbon dioxide is going to cause the apocalypse, Jeffrey thought. But then he reminded himself he was representing his school, and he did his best to remain calm. "As I told you before, our honor code is a code of behavior. Everyone that wishes to attend our school is expected to follow the same standards. It's all equal. We discriminate against no one."

"Your truth-capable privilege has made you blind," Ms. Hursh said.

"What in the world does that even mean?" Jeffrey asked, starting to lose his cool. *Perfect messenger? I'll show Scott a perfect messenger.*

Professor Carroll held up a hand. "Let me try to explain," she said. "What you seem to not understand is that there are parts of your honor code that some students cannot choose to follow."

"They can't choose to follow some of our standards?"

"No."

"Are they robots?"

"Of course not! We're talking about students!"

"Okay, well if they aren't robots, then they can choose to follow our standards."

"No, Jeffrey," Professor Carroll said. "No, they can't."

"So they're robots, then?"

"No! They're not robots! They're humans just like you and me, and they deserve the same respect as you and me!"

"Robots deserve the same respect as you and me?"

"We're not talking about robots!"

"Are you sure? I did a project on robots when I was an undergrad. They just follow their programming. They don't really have a choice. But people have a choice. They can choose if they want to follow our standards or not."

"They can't choose to follow your standards because doing so would be denying a core part of themselves!" Professor Carroll said. "You are denying their humanity! You are asking them to be mute! You don't expect yourself to be mute, yet you demand that they be mute! They can't choose to not be human. They can't choose to not be themselves!"

And that was it. Jeffrey was fed up with the nonsense. Were these people even speaking English? "Okay, stop being so vague. What in the world are you talking about? Who are we discriminating against? What is this rule in our honor code that you think is so horrible?"

The three members of the Northeast Accreditation Commission looked at each other for a moment. Then Professor Carroll answered him. "The problem is that your school forbids lying."

Jeffrey stared at Professor Carroll. "I'm sorry," he said. "Could you repeat that?"

Professor Carroll folded her arms and leaned forward on the table. She spoke slowly. "BYU's honor code forbids lying. That's the problem. The problem is your policy against lying."

"Our policy against lying? What's wrong with our policy against lying?"

"It discriminates against the must-lies."

"The must-lies?"

"Yes, the must-lies, those who *must* lie. You can't require them to be honest. Telling them they have to be honest is like telling them they cannot be who they are. For you, lying seems like just a behavior that can be chosen or not chosen, but it only seems that way to you because of your truth-capable privilege. What you need to understand is that telling a must-lie to not lie is like telling them to not breathe."

"It's nothing at all like telling someone to not breathe!" Jeffrey said. "If someone doesn't breathe, they'll die!"

"Yes," Professor Carroll said. "It's exactly like that."

"No, I'm pretty sure it's not."

"We're talking about communication, Jeffrey, communication! What could be more central to human identity than communication? It's a necessity of life!"

"So is peeing," Jeffrey said, no longer caring that he was representing his school. "But that doesn't mean I should just whip it out and pee whenever I please."

"How predictable that you would bring that up!" Ms. Hursh said.

"Mr. Bruder!" Professor Carroll said. "Your crudeness is entirely unjustified. You don't understand what you're saying. For must-lies, lying is part of their very existence. To deny them the right to lie is to deny them the right to *be*."

Jeffrey laughed at her. "That's got be one of the stupidest things I've ever heard. You could take any of our standards, declare that a certain group of people *have* to break it, and then demand that we throw that standard out and not teach against the behavior. Either right and wrong exist, or right and wrong don't exist. But if right and wrong exist, then some people are going to want to do wrong, and some people are going to be upset when we tell them that what they want to do is wrong."

"It's immoral to moralize," Ms. Hursh said.

Jeffrey grunted in shock. "Are you even listening to yourself?"

"It's all very scientific!" Professor Carroll said. "Must-lies are people who *must* lie. Lying is who they are and we need to affirm that fact. Oh, I wish Professor Murray were here. He's a must-lie. I wish you could hear directly from him how rules like your honor code affect must-lies. Ms. Hursh, why did Professor Murray claim he couldn't come today?"

"He said his car broke down on the freeway."

"That's right. Which means he is probably home taking a nap. You see, Jeffrey, for people like Professor Murray, lying is simply part of their nature. It would be wrong for us to expect anything different from him. We must affirm him and celebrate the diversity he brings to our commission."

Jeffrey held his hands up. "Listen, you can celebrate whatever you want, but BYU is a Mormon school, and we have a right to base our standards on what Mormons consider to be right and wrong; and we believe that lying is wrong. That's why our honor code requires students to be honest."

"You can preach your beliefs of right and wrong in your church," Professor Carroll said, "but BYU is a university, and universities are not allowed to discriminate, which is why your honor code needs to change. Must-lies are who they are. They are people who *must* lie."

"But you could say that about any behavior you wanted to force people to accept!"

"Don't be ridiculous. Must-lies are a special case."

"No, lying is just a behavior like anything else. Must-lies claim that they *are* that behavior and now we're suddenly forced to accept the behavior and pretend there's nothing wrong with it. Hey, what if I say that I *am* a polluter. Filling the air with apocalyptic greenhouse gas is part of the core of my existence. I was born to drive an SUV with zero passengers. You can't tell me to watch my carbon footprint anymore because telling me that is like telling me to deny who I am. See what I mean? You could say that about any behavior. Everyone has their own definition of sin. Worrying about carbon is no different than worrying about lying."

"No, we worry about carbon because pollution affects everyone else."

"So does lying! It's moral pollution. No one is an island. The actions of one affect the actions of another. Like I said, we all have our own definition of sin, and worrying about carbon is no different than worrying about lying."

"No, it's completely different," Professor Carroll said. "Lying is only prohibited for religious reasons, but our concern about carbon is completely logical. It's all very scientific! Do you think Professor Walsh would be holding his breath right now if the scientific consensus didn't tell him to?"

Professor Walsh nodded vigorously and gave two thumbs up, his face turning a pale shade of blue as he suffered through his coffee penance.

"You can't compare things like that because they are completely different," Professor Carroll said. "Must-lies are actual people, not some theoretical construct you dream up to try and justify your discrimination of others. Discrimination is always wrong."

Part of Jeffrey wanted to continue to reason with them even though they had shown little evidence of being influenced by reason. "Why did you call BYU here if not to threaten to rescind our accreditation unless we stop discriminating against lying, but if you rescind our accreditation because we discriminate against lying, then you would be discriminating yourselves, and I thought you just said that discrimination is always wrong?"

"It's not wrong to discriminate against discrimination," Ms. Hursh said.

Professor Walsh nodded. His penance was apparently complete as he was now gulping air, his face slowly returning to normal.

"So you say it's not wrong to discriminate against discrimination because the act of discrimination itself is wrong?" Jeffrey asked.

"Exactly," Ms. Hursh said.

"So basically," Jeffrey said, "it's wrong to discriminate against actions that *I* think are wrong, but it's not wrong to discriminate against actions that *you* think are wrong?"

Professor Carroll replied, "Discrimination is wrong, period. We only discriminate against those who discriminate because society needs to learn to stop doing it."

Jeffrey smiled. "So, if it's okay to discriminate against those who discriminate, does that mean it's okay for me to discriminate against those who discriminate against those who discriminate?"

"Yes," said Professor Carroll.

"No!" said Ms. Hursh.

"Oh, my!" Professor Walsh said, still panting. "Oh, my!"

Ms. Hursh scowled at Jeffrey. "Stop being microaggressive."

"What does that even mean?" Jeffrey said, throwing up his hands.

"Ah! Wonderful!" Professor Walsh said, sounding genuinely excited as he turned to Ms. Hursh. "I've been trying hard to identify microaggressions, but it's difficult for me. I'm sure it's just my white-male privilege getting in the way. Could you please point out how he was being microaggressive, so I can better understand and avoid it myself?"

Ms. Hursh transferred her scowl to Professor Walsh. "I don't recall the exact reason," she said, "but he made me feel uncomfortable and feeling uncomfortable is a sure sign of microaggression."

Professor Walsh frowned, the gears in his head moving slowly. "I'm sorry, but that's not very helpful."

And Ms. Hursh absolutely exploded. "Helpful? Why is it my job to be helpful to you? Is it because I'm a woman? Am I supposed to just help any man who asks? What am I, some sort of universal 'helpmeet' for every man?"

"Oh, my! Certainly not! I'm just doing my best here, Ms. Hursh. I'm just trying to do the right thing, but how can I do the right thing if I don't know what the right thing is? It's very frustrating!"

Professor Carroll put a soft hand on his arm. "It's not about your white-male feelings. You need to defer to the perceptions of the unempowered."

"Oh, my! Oh, my! You're quite right!" Professor Walsh clasped his hands together. "Oh, my! I shouldn't have said you are right because that implies I am in a position to judge you are right. How wrong of me!" He grabbed his hair, ready to pull it out. "Oh, my! Oh, my! I just implied that I, a white male, am in a position to judge myself. How wrong of me!" He shook his head, hands still clutching his hair. "Oh, my! Oh, my! I just can't stop myself. Please,

Professor Carroll. I must do penance before I make this worse. Please! Tell me what the appropriate penance is for this."

Professor Carroll patted his arm. "Of course, Professor Walsh. You try so hard. You really do." She opened her leather book again, flipping through pages until she came to the one she was looking for. "Now, let's see," she said. "What rating on the sexism scale would you say that was?"

Professor Walsh turned a fearful glance to Ms. Hursh, apparently too scared to even open his mouth.

"Alpha Five at a minimum," Ms. Hursh said. "And you have to intersect his white-male-truth-capable privilege as well."

"Yes, yes, Ms. Hursh. It's not my first time at the scales." Professor Carroll fiddled with her scale for a moment, loading various weights on both sides.

"Alpha Five? Oh, my! That's very serious. Oh, my! I just made it worse. Oh, my! Saying I made it worse just made it worse and I just did it again. Please, Professor Carroll, please. What's my penance for an Alpha Five sexist remark?"

"Hmm ... looks like ten lashes. Self-imposed, of course."

"Oh, my! Of course. Of course." Professor Walsh pushed his chair back from the table and stood up. He looked to the ground from side to side and then turned sheepishly to Professor Carroll. "I forgot my whip. Do you happen to have one I can borrow?"

"Yes," Professor Carroll said. Then she pulled out a small brown leather whip from her bag. It appeared to be a matching set with her leather book of dogma.

"You call that a whip?" Ms. Hursh scoffed. "Here, use mine." She handed Professor Walsh a black leather whip, small chunks of metal attached to its tips. Jeffrey could see dried blood on the sharp edges.

Professor Walsh took the whip and laid it on the table in front of him, spreading it out to its full length. It was as long as a man's arm. He touched the sharp metal barbs gently. "Has it been sterilized?"

"Do you deserve for it to have been sterilized?" asked Ms. Hursh.

"Oh, my! No! You're quite right. I positively reek of privilege. It disgusts me." He picked up the whip, pushing his chair farther back behind him.

"Can I leave my sweater on?"

"If it doesn't pierce skin, then it never happened," Ms. Hursh replied, looking eager.

"Oh, my! Excellent point." He pulled his sweater up over his head, exposing pathetic rolls of pasty white skin. Then he closed his eyes and held the whip out in front of him. Jeffrey grimaced in anticipation.

"One!" Professor Walsh swung the whip over his shoulder, the leather making a cracking sound against his back. He jumped a little and let out a soft squeak at the impact. Then he slowly drew the whip back in front of himself.

"Two!"

Little drops of blood were flung onto the table when he brought the whip forward again.

"Can you please stop doing that?" Jeffrey asked, trying unsuccessfully to look away.

"Quiet," Professor Carroll said. "He's doing his penance."

"Three!"

Professor Walsh was huffing now, his face full of pain.

"Wincing shows that you lack remorse," Ms. Hursh said. "Maybe you haven't checked all your privilege after all."

"Four!"

Jeffrey could almost feel the barbs of the whip tearing into flesh.

"Five!"

Professor Walsh pulled the whip back, slower this time, more and more drops of blood falling onto the table.

"That's really disturbing," Jeffrey said.

Professor Walsh opened his eyes, face frozen in an attempt to hide the pain. "Why? Is it because I'm overweight?"

Jeffrey gaped at the half-naked man. "It's not that," Jeffrey said. "Well it is that. But it's not that. It's just that ... please stop doing that!"

"You're fat-shaming me!" Professor Walsh said, leaning against the table as he gasped for air. His thick shoulders showed thin red lines above where the whip had struck his back.

"No, I'm just not a fan of watching someone self-flagellate."

Ms. Hursh cleared her throat. "Being fat-shamed doesn't absolve you of your penance," she said.

"Quite right," Professor Walsh said. He swung the whip again. "Six!"

Jeffrey looked away.

"Seven!"

"You can borrow my whip after him if you'd like," Ms. Hursh said to Jeffrey. "To pay penance for your fat-shaming."

Jeffrey thought she sounded a little too excited at the idea. "Oh, I'm quite alright. Thanks."

"Eight!"

"Almost there!" Professor Carroll said, cheering him on.

"Nine!"

"Ten!"

He collapsed forward, dropping the whip to the table as he leaned hard against it, the table moving forward a few inches under his weight. Ms. Hursh collected her whip, running a finger along the fresh blood before putting it away in her purse. Then Professor Carroll stood up to help Professor Walsh back into his sweater.

"You're an inspiration to us all," she told him. "I don't know what I'd do if I had as much privilege to work through as you do."

"Oh, my!" Professor Walsh said, unable to say anything more. "Oh, my!" His face pale, he sank into his chair. Then he jerked forward after his fresh wounds touched the seat's back.

"Do you whip yourself for all your sins?" Jeffrey asked, too disturbed by the spectacle to say anything sarcastic.

"Not sins!" Ms. Hursh said. "None of your foolish religious dogma here! Not sins!"

"Definitely not," agreed Professor Carroll. "It's all very scientific! Not sins at all."

"Then what do you call them?" Jeffrey asked. "What do you call things like fat-shaming?"

"Those are things that thou shalt not do." Professor Carroll said.

"Things that thou shalt not do?"

"That's right. Things that thou shalt not do," she repeated.

"So, basically … sins," Jeffrey said.

"No!" Ms. Hursh said. "Not sins! None of your foolish religious dogma!"

"They aren't sins," Professor Carroll said. "They are things that thou shalt not do."

"It sounds to me like we're talking about the same thing."

"No, we're not," Professor Carroll said. "This is completely different. It's all very scientific!"

"I'm sure it is," Jeffrey said, regaining his sarcasm now that color was returning to Professor Walsh's face.

"Did we talk about their speech code yet?" Ms. Hursh asked her two colleagues. "They need to ban any discouragement of lying. Preaching against lying is hate speech."

Jeffrey had been so disturbed by the latest ritual that it took him a moment to recall the prior conversation. "Speech code? Hate speech? No … just no. Listen, I have a small message to deliver. It should clear all this up—"

"I think requiring a speech code right now might be too large of a step," Professor Carroll said, ignoring Jeffrey. "We can't expect BYU to switch overnight from being a discriminating campus to being a completely affirming campus. Banning any opinions against lying can come next. First, however, they need to get rid of their requirement for honesty."

"What? No!" Jeffrey said. "We're not going to do that. As I already told you, we aren't discriminating against anyone. We don't care if they call themselves must-lies. We don't care if they want to lie. Lots of people want to do all kinds of wrong things; there's nothing special about that. What we care about is what they choose. We require everyone to be honest because lying is wrong."

"Oh, my!" Professor Walsh said, his voice sounding as if it was painful to talk.

"Oh, my, what? Lying is wrong. Some might disagree, but this isn't their school. Let them start their own school if they want to permit, encourage, or celebrate lying."

Professor Carroll shook her head. "Jeffrey, what you're saying is that some people—some people *themselves*—are wrong."

"No, I'm saying that lying—the action of lying—is wrong."

"But, Jeffrey, you aren't listening to what I'm telling you. Lying is in their nature. You can't just tell them to not lie."

"Why not? You just told me to not do something. Why can't I tell others to not do something?"

"Because lying is who they are!"

"Really? Well what if scolding is who *I* am? What if I was born to scold others?"

"Stop being ridiculous," Professor Carroll said.

"That's not very affirming of my identity as a scolder."

"Stop being ridiculous!"

"I wish Professor Murray were here," Professor Walsh said, his voice still sounding wounded. "Maybe Jeffrey would understand it better if he heard it straight from a must-lie. If only Professor Murray's car didn't break down ..."

Ms. Hursh snorted. "His car didn't break down."

"But he said it did," Professor Walsh replied. "He said that, and I was assuming he was telling the—"

Ms. Hursh slammed her hand down on the table. "Telling the what?" she yelled. "Telling the truth? Why would you assume that? Why would he do that?"

Professor Walsh paled again. "Oh, my! I just thought it was better to assume—"

"Better to assume he was telling the truth?" Ms. Hursh spat. "I can't believe you just said that. How disgustingly truth-normative."

"Oh, my! I didn't think of that! I'm so blinded by my truth-capable privilege. Oh, my!" Professor Walsh reached for the whip again, which Ms. Hursh had quietly placed back on the table.

"I don't think that will be necessary," Professor Carroll said, grabbing Professor Walsh's arm and setting it back down on the table. "We all have a lot to learn."

Jeffrey shook his head in disgust. "Professor Walsh, if you were caught by a cannibal tribe, you'd scrub out the cook pot for them, wouldn't you?"

"Cannibal tribe? Scrub out the cook pot?" Professor Walsh still looked flustered. "I don't rightfully know. Are these hypothetical cannibals people of color?"

"What!" Ms. Hursh yelled. "How dare you!"

Professor Walsh winced. "I was just trying to determine if we were talking about an empowered group of people or not."

"But think what you're implying," Professor Carroll said, looking a little disturbed herself.

"Oh, my! Oh, my!" Professor Walsh reached down and grabbed his sweater as if he were about to take it off again.

"Wow, look at the time!" Jeffrey said loudly, slapping his hands on his knees and leaning forward as if he were once again about to stand up. "Like I said, I have a message to deliver to you, the message is—"

"You're not leaving without agreeing to a new speech code!" Ms. Hursh demanded.

Professor Carroll shook a finger at her. "I told you it's too soon for a speech code! First, they need to stop punishing people for lying. Punishing people for telling others to not lie can come later."

"No!" Jeffrey said. "No, no, a million times no! Listen, all of you! Pull all the academic goop out of your ears and listen to reason for once! Lying is behavior! Okay? Lying is behavior, and we ban lots of wrong behavior. We don't allow cheating. Should we allow that? We don't allow stealing either. Should we allow that?"

"That's completely different," Professor Carroll said. "We're talking about students' identities here. BYU needs to affirm everyone's identity!"

"What a complete load of—oh, I'm sorry but I can't finish that sentence. Do you know why I can't finish that sentence? Because our honor code prohibits swearing. It doesn't matter how much you deserve it. It doesn't matter how much I want to do it. What matters is that I choose not to. These are actions. These are behaviors. These are things that we have as much right to expect people to not do as you have the right to expect us to not expect people to not do them. The identity thing is BS. People are not their wants and desires. If I like to scold people, can I call myself a scolder and forbid you from telling me not to scold? If I like to cheat, can I call myself a cheater and forbid you from telling me not to cheat?"

"We've told you again and again," Professor Carroll said, her voice rising. "That's completely different. Must-lies *must* lie! It's all very scientific! You can't ask them to not lie. That's asking them to be mute their entire life. That's wrong, Jeffrey! It's wrong for BYU to tell people that lying is wrong! Stop bringing up these disrespectful comparisons that have nothing to do with what we're talking about!"

"They have everything to do with what we're talking about! Here, how about this." Jeffrey turned to Professor Walsh. "Professor Walsh, you seem like a very nice man, perhaps a little bit too nice, but a very nice man nevertheless. But, Professor Walsh, you really need to lose a few pounds."

The three members of the accreditation commission gasped in unison.

"You just fat-shamed him!" Professor Carroll said, her face red with anger.

Jeffrey threw his arms in the air. "So what! You can't tell me not to fat-shame. I'm a fat-shamer! It's my identity. I can't *not* fat-shame! You can't expect me to not do it!"

"That's completely different!"

"No it's not! Fat-shaming is an action just like lying is an action, and now that fat-shaming is part of my identity, you can't tell me to not fat-shame anymore!"

"That's completely different!"

"How is that in any way different?"

"Because that's something *we* think is a sin!"

And the whole room paused for a moment. Then, Jeffrey broke the silence. "Don't you mean 'things that thou shalt not do'?"

"Oh, whatever," Professor Carroll said.

The door behind Jeffrey opened, and the woman from before stepped back into the room. "I'm sorry to disturb you all," she said, "but I just wanted to remind you that we'll be turning off the power in ten minutes in observance of Earth Hour. So if you need to use the elevators to get downstairs, I suggest you do so now. I've been told that the stairwells will be dark as well." Then she left the room.

Jeffrey stood up. "And with that, it's time for my message." He held his hands out toward Professor Carroll and Ms. Hursh. "Ladies," he said. Ms. Hursh growled in response. "Gentleman," Jeffrey said, gesturing at Professor Walsh. "The message I was asked to deliver is simple: You are the Northeast Accreditation Commission, but BYU is not in the northeast. I pity the schools that are, but BYU is not one of them, and therefore I bid you adieu."

Jeffrey turned and walked toward the door, the three members of the Northeast Accreditation Commission talking hurriedly to each other.

"Utah isn't in the northeast?"

"BYU is in Utah? I thought it was in Pennsylvania."

"Why Pennsylvania?"

"Isn't that where the Amish live?"

And then Jeffrey walked out the door, the nonsense of the Northeast Accreditation Commission fading into nothing. Oh, that all nonsense could be left behind so easily!

Invest in Oxygen Masks

ALL YOU HAVE TO DO IS STOP BY MY PLACE twice a day and feed Princess."

Abby cradled her cell phone between her shoulder and her ear, her hands on the steering wheel, her eyes on the road.

"No, you don't need to let her out. She uses the dog door."

There hadn't been any other cars on the highway since Abby exited the freeway and headed north.

"No, you can't take Princess to your apartment. Ralphster would eat her! ... Yes, he would! He's a vicious dog. ... Yes, he is! Don't you remember what he did to that squirrel?"

A large warning sign was coming up on her right.

"No, you can't just move in to my place. We already talked about this!"

Abby passed the warning sign. Something about the air? She didn't remember that from her last visit.

"I don't care if it'd be easier to take care of Princess that way. We already talked about this. You know my requirement. I'm not going to budge. ... Yes, it's a big step, but so is moving in together."

Abby laughed.

"Oh, you say that, but I know you wouldn't really want us to, even if you pretend otherwise. You'd rather wait."

Abby laughed again. She passed another warning sign. This one was larger. The signs were definitely saying something about the air. Was there a problem with pollution? Sheryl hadn't mentioned anything.

"Listen, I have to go. I'm almost to Sheryl's town. ... Yes, I know Princess is annoying, but she used to be my mom's dog. I can't just get rid of her. ... No, you can't leave her at a park and hope a nice family takes her home! Don't you realize that little annoying dog is my only inheritance? All of my mom's retirement funds went into her medical care. ... No, Princess isn't worth any money. It's sentimental value. ... Oh, you wouldn't understand."

A blinking sign ahead warned her to slow down. Abby definitely didn't remember that one. She relaxed her foot on the gas, her car slowing to half speed.

"Besides, she's chipped. They'd just bring her back to my place anyway, like the monkey's paw or whatever that story was. ... Okay, maybe it was a different story then, but you know what I mean."

Her phone beeped, another call coming in.

"Ah, that's probably Sheryl on the other line. I gotta go. I'll call you tonight. ... Love ya, babe."

Juggling the phone in one hand, Abby switched to the incoming call.

"Sheryl? Hi! ... Yes, I'm almost to your town. Hey, what's the story with the warning signs? ... I'm about a mile away. ... Yes, I see the big black things coming up.

What are those, some sort of buildings? ... What's that noise? It's like some giant fan or a vacuum or something."

Abby watched the approaching structures nervously. The vacuum sound was getting louder and louder. She could barely hear Sheryl on the phone.

"Wait, what? ... Yes, of course my seat belt is buckled. Why would you ask that?"

Then she passed by the giant structures, the enormous sucking sound drowning out the conversation entirely, and as soon as she passed them, her car swerved to the left as if hit by a powerful pull of wind. Abby immediately gasped, the air suddenly gone. She was choking! She dropped the cell phone, her car swerving again, and everything went black ...

Her car door was open, and Sheryl was strapping something plastic to Abby's face.

"What's going on?" Abby asked, blinking in confusion. She looked at Sheryl, who was wearing a clear plastic mask herself, a small tube running down to something in her purse. Then Abby noticed her own mask was connected to a tube as well. Sheryl handed her a small canister.

"Here," Sheryl told her. "You can hold it in your purse like I do."

The loud sucking noise made it difficult to hear.

"What's going on?" Abby repeated, speaking loudly. "Why are we wearing oxygen masks? What are those giant black things? Why does it sound like your town is being vacuumed up?"

"Let's walk to my place and I'll explain on the way," Sheryl said.

Abby was about to suggest they drive instead, but then she looked around and realized she had driven her car into a ditch. She'd have to be towed out.

"Come on," Sheryl said. "It's a short walk. We'll come back for your car later."

Abby stood up with Sheryl's help. The oxygen coming through her mask had a funny smell to it. Abby wondered if it was from the canister. They stumbled out of the ditch and then started walking along the side of the road. Then they stepped up onto the sidewalk as they entered the town on its main thoroughfare.

"What's going on, Sheryl?" Abby asked. She stuffed her oxygen canister into her purse. "Why are we wearing oxygen masks?"

Sheryl adjusted the strap of her mask. Then she pulled out her canister, checking a reading. "Do you remember when I told you about that billionaire moving to our town?"

"Yeah, you said something to me about him last year."

"Right, well, as soon as he moved in, he started buying up all the property on the outskirts of town. Everyone was excited at first. We thought he'd do something great, put our town on the map somehow, you know? But then he installed these giant machines all around town and started to suck out all the oxygen. We've had to wear oxygen masks ever since."

"Why would he want to suck the oxygen out of your town?"

Sheryl shrugged. "Who knows? He's a little eccentric."

The shops along the main road were all open like normal, men and women going about their daily chores with oxygen masks on their faces.

"I don't get it," Abby said. "Why do you let him suck all the oxygen out of your town? Why don't you try to stop him?"

"We did try," Sheryl said. "We all complained about it, so the town council made a law that it was illegal to suck oxygen out of the town."

"Then why is he still doing it?"

"Because he took us to court, and the judge threw out our new law. Apparently it lacked a rational basis, so it was unconstitutional. That's what the judge said, anyway."

"What? How could it lack a rational basis? Humans need oxygen to live!"

"That's what we told the judge!" Sheryl said. "But he just waved it away like it was nothing. He said that people go without oxygen in the air all the time—scuba divers, military jet pilots, astronauts. He said that if some people can go without oxygen in the air around them, then obviously having oxygen in the air isn't actually necessary, and therefore he declared that the law lacked a rational justification and was unconstitutional."

"What? Humans need oxygen to breathe! Your law was just reflecting that fact!"

"Sure, but he rejected that reason. He said we needed a better one."

"But that *is* the reason! What else are you supposed to say?"

"I don't know. We've always had oxygen in the air to breathe. I never really thought we'd have to defend something so obvious."

Abby shook her head, the plastic oxygen mask swaying a little from side to side. "None of this makes any sense."

"Do you really think so? I thought it didn't make any sense either, but the media keep talking like it makes complete sense. I was wondering if maybe it was just me that was mixed up."

A jogger passed them, running along the side of the road, a large oxygen tank strapped to his back.

Sheryl went on. "But it's like you said. We need oxygen in the air to breathe. That *is* the reason. But if the judge already rejected the reason, what do we do then? Come up with a lesser reason? Why would that be more effective than the actual reason? Besides, at some point, I think you have to realize that some judges simply want to let eccentric billionaires suck oxygen out of our air, so no matter what reason you come up with, those judges will work up an excuse to rule the way they want to rule."

Abby shook her head again. "This just makes no sense. If something is necessary for survival, then that's rational! People need oxygen in the air to live. It's perfectly rational to base a law on that fact. Sure, there are corner cases, but that doesn't change the main truth. Focusing on the corner cases is irrational."

"Yeah," Sheryl said. "You know, after the judge ruled the law unconstitutional, an analogy keeps coming to my mind."

"What's that?"

"Imagine you tell a toddler to not touch a hot stove because it will burn their hand," Sheryl said, "but instead of listening to you, the toddler turns around and says 'because it will burn their hand' isn't a good reason and to give them another one or else they'll put their hand on the stove. What do you say to that? What do you say when the actual reason has been rejected?"

"I don't know, but why are toddlers controlling the conversation?"

"I don't know!"

"Craziness," Abby said.

"I agree. Craziness."

A woman crossed the street in front of them, walking a terrier. There was a small oxygen mask strapped to the dog's face.

"And the judge thinks this is rational?" Abby asked.

"I guess so."

"Well, what if it's the judges that are being irrational? What if irrational judges are declaring that rational laws are irrational? What do we do then?"

Sheryl looked at her friend and shrugged. "Invest in oxygen masks."

Melvin the Protester

O N TUESDAY AFTERNOON AT 4:37 P.M. Mountain Standard Time, Melvin's life finally began. Exiting his place of work, he stepped out onto the sidewalk and that's when he saw her—*her*, the woman his life had been waiting for. And now his life could begin because there she was—average frame, medium-length black hair, attractive face—holding a fist in the air as she marched down the middle of the street in the front of a large, loud crowd. Where had she been all his life?

Melvin dropped his computer case to the pavement and rushed into the street to be near her. The crowd was chanting. They were yelling. They were speaking some sort of truth to some sort of power, and now Melvin was part of it! And she was in the front of it all, only feet away, her straight, fine hair spilling over the black-and-white kef-fiyeh wrapped around her delicate neck. And there Melvin was, he the avatar of all passive men desperate for the kind of meaning that can only be provided by one such as she, she the embodiment of a million strong, independent female protagonists compressed into one perfect diamond amidst a crowd of rough, smelly, generally hostile faces. He knew more than he had ever known anything before: he had found his soul mate.

Yes! This is life! he thought, his heart rising at the sight of her and at the yelling and the chanting. This was what he had been missing! He had never felt so involved. He couldn't hold it in anymore. He had to express himself.

"I'm very troubled!" he shouted. It was liberating to care about such an important cause. He imagined his fellow marchers nodding approvingly as they continued their own yelling. Some in the front were waving signs as well. He couldn't read them from behind, but he was sure they were brilliant. How great it was to be a part of this, whatever it was!

The protesters continued down the street, making their way to an intersection where they stopped, blocking traffic in all directions. Melvin shook his fist at the vague faces behind the windshields of waiting cars. Your daily commutes, your grocery trips, they aren't as important as our very, very important cause! He felt himself pulled higher in the euphoria of being within something greater than himself.

Loosening his tie, he yelled, "I'm so, so, somewhat angry about all this!" It felt right. He lost himself in the moment and let it all go.

"I hate whatever everyone else here hates!" he screamed, waving his arms in the air. And she was there in the front, her fist still held high, defying the laws of gravity and the weariness of the flesh. Every inch of her screamed perfection, at least the inches he could see, and he was sure the other inches were great as well. How could it be otherwise? And in the beauty of her eyes and the rhythm of her chants, any desire for gainful employment or semblance of productivity fell away like skin flaking off a sunburn.

Then they were marching again, weaving their way through the traffic down one street, banging on the cars as they went, yelling and chanting and singing about their glorious struggle. Melvin patted the hood of a BMW, careful not to leave a smudge. He waved at the old woman inside, who looked frightened of the crowd. She shouldn't be frightened, he thought. She should be in awe of their grand purpose! They were marching for justice, adjective justice. Melvin didn't know what the adjective was, but he was sure it was something impressive!

And so he marched in lockstep with the rest of the protesters. He was one of them now. Already, he had made out an Amazon shopping cart in his mind. First, he would click to buy a Guy Fawkes mask. Then his mouse would say "Yes, Amazon, I would like a Che Guevara shirt. Large size, please!" He'd skip the keffiyeh because scarves look better on the ladies, but he'd definitely add an iPhone to his shopping cart, an iPhone to take pictures of his brave stand against whatever it was they were standing against. And with a click of his phone's touch screen, those pictures would be proudly shared online for all the world to see: on Facebook, on Twitter, on Instagram, maybe even on Google+—that's how important his pictures would be!

The crowd had worked its way through the waiting cars and were walking along the open street again, bystanders pointing at them from the sidewalks and doorways. Melvin smiled a euphoric smile, reveling in his presence among the protesters. It felt good to be standing for something. It felt good to be seen standing for something—something important, something essential, something a tad unclear yet surely monumental. People were watching. Cameras were rolling. He might be on the news tomorrow! "Previously Obscure Local Man Joins Grand Protest!" That's what the headlines would say. And the pictures would show him—and her too, a wide enough shot to include them both, maybe some of the more amiable-looking protesters as well. There were a few, here and there.

A quarter of the group split off and charged into a liquor store. Melvin wished they had visited the bookstore next door instead. He had no need for alcohol; he was drunk on true love! And now with his dream in sight, he could really use a self-help book about first dates. But sadly, none of his fellow protesters seemed interested in expressing their frustration amongst the book aisles. Oh, well, he'd add a dating book to his Amazon shopping cart along with his protest gear; and, thanks to his annual Prime membership, it'd be delivered in time for a weekend date!

He imagined himself waiting on his front porch for the delivery. His tools of resistance and love would arrive efficiently boxed, but somehow the UPS delivery man would know what was inside, and he'd give Melvin a knowing look, as if to say, "Wow." Melvin, for his part, would just look back at the delivery man, not saying anything, but by not saying anything he'd actually be saying, "That's right— Wow. I'm part of an important movement. Maybe, if you play your cards right, you'll be part of an important movement someday as well."

Back in reality, Melvin removed his tie and let it fall to the ground as he continued his march down the street. The crowd grew smaller and smaller as more of its members broke off to visit the various retail establishments on each side. But not the bookstore? Doesn't anyone care about bookstores? Oh, well, let the looters loot, Melvin thought. We are the ones with our hearts set for the cause, whatever that cause might be! And she was still there of course, his beautiful angel of destruction, her fist still raised in the air as if to say, "Yes, Melvin, I've been waiting for you, too."

Everything was so clear to Melvin now. He knew he'd never be happy today until today's outrage was defeated, and he'd never be happy tomorrow until tomorrow's outrage was defeated, and the next day, and the next, and he got a little bit weary just thinking about the unending monotony, yet he felt energized as well because she would be there beside him, or at least a little bit in front of him, and they'd be fighting against whatever the day's outrage might be, refusing to be happy until ... until ... never mind until—she'd be there, and he'd be there with her, or at least somewhat close to her!

The crowd stopped for a moment to turn and yell at a building that was guilty of something truly awful. Then they resumed their marching, each of the protesters reaching down and picking up a rock as they went. Melvin picked up a rock as well, a rock of justice, justice for whatever it was they were marching for. He felt more alive than he had previously thought possible, as if his id were there in his hand and he was holding it and about to do something with it, something important—he could feel it!

They turned the corner and saw a large group of police officers blocking the road. Holy crap, the police are wearing riot gear! Holy crap, we're throwing rocks at them! That seemed a little too aggressive for Melvin so, while he did raise his rock in solidarity with his brothers and sisters in arms, he let the rock fall discretely to the ground as he swung his arm and pretended to throw. Did she see me? No, he told himself, relieved. She was too busy yelling at the police officers, who were advancing on the group.

Melvin yelled along with her. He had run out of ideas for sentences, so he just made up words and yelled them at the top of his voice. No one could hear him anyway. An officer was saying something on a bullhorn. The protesters shouted in response. More rocks were thrown.

Then a tear gas canister hit the ground next to Melvin and he immediately started to choke, his eyes burning. Clutching his face, he looked to his lover, fearful she might be in pain as well. He was grateful to see her hurriedly donning a gas mask. Did anyone bring an extra one? No? One more item for my Amazon shopping cart then, Melvin thought as he squeezed his eyes shut to keep out the pain, but before he had closed them, she had looked in his direction. Was that a wink? Was that a smile?

And he was down on the pavement, coughing, crying tears of pain mixed with tears of joy. Hands grabbed his arms, twisting them behind his back. He looked up, hoping to see her beautiful face, but he saw the face of a police officer wearing a gas mask instead.

"It's smoke, not tear gas," the officer said, but Melvin's eyes disagreed. If it was smoke, then it was extra tearful smoke, he was sure! Something plastic was drawn tight across his wrists, and he was hauled to his feet. He couldn't see her, but she was out there somewhere, somewhere in the mists of justice and love, fighting for whatever it was they were fighting for.

Maybe she'd be arrested too. Maybe she'd be put in the same police van. They'd smile at each other on the way to the station. They wouldn't speak—such passionate love needs no words. But immediately after posting bail they'd find each other and from then on till forever they'd always be together. He could see it now. Picnics in the park. Her black-and-white keffiyeh spread out on the ground under them like a blanket, the two of them sitting side by side, discussing deep meaningful things about how the world needs to change in deep meaningful ways.

Yes, the two of them would always be together, and life would be perfect, just perfect—but not too perfect; otherwise they wouldn't have something to protest against.

Killing the Golem

SKINHEADS? WHAT ARE THOSE RACIST worms doing walking on the street in broad daylight? Armando scowled at their three backs through the dust cloud that choked the street, the middle skinhead large and strong, obviously their leader, a nervous toady to each side, the three of them half a block ahead and walking in the same direction Armando was going. He muttered a curse into his dust mask. Skinheads meant trouble. Skinheads always meant trouble. And I don't need trouble today, he said to himself.

Twenty-five minutes to his shop. Thirty minutes before the next patrol. What are the skinheads thinking? Armando wondered. Are they suicidal or just stupid? He wiped the excess dust from his goggles as a rusty car drove past, armed guards on horseback riding before and after. The streets were full of people, walkers like Armando hurrying along crumbling sidewalks, their faces protected against the dust, while carriages, horses, and the occasional car braved the potholed streets.

Busy streets and between patrols—that's why Armando had chosen to run his errand now. It was a dust day too, a perfect time to sneak a shipment to his shop. But he hadn't planned on running into any skinheads. Why would he have? Skinheads never dared be in public anymore. Of all the days for them to suddenly get brave, Armando thought, why did it have to be today? He cursed again into his dust mask.

Pausing at an intersection, Armando allowed a group of horseback riders to pass, their black jackets and pants now tan with a fine layer of dust. Then he hurried across the street, dodging between a wagon and a dust-covered van. Vehicles rarely slowed for pedestrians anymore, especially not on dust days.

Back on the sidewalk, he checked again on the skinheads, hoping they had turned down a side street; but they were still there ahead of him and still moving in the same direction. Turn, you worms, Armando muttered. Turn! Why won't they turn? He cursed again, loudly enough to earn a glare from a passing woman. Armando ignored her.

Twenty minutes to his shop. Twenty-five minutes until the next patrol. Armando didn't have enough cash for a bribe, not after that last-minute price gouge by Olaf. Clever, Armando thought, very clever. Olaf had known that Armando had a tight window and there was no time for haggling. That cleverness had won Olaf a twenty-five percent premium over their agreed upon price. Well, we'll see how clever you are next time, Armando thought, the gears in his head already turning about how to get his money back. He always got it back, one way or another. He'd get it back, and he'd teach Olaf to never be so clever again, not with him.

Armando crossed another street. Then another. Still the skinheads kept moving in the same direction, their leader practically strutting, his head held high, as he walked up the street. Armando had never seen such arrogance in a skinhead since the golem had been created. It made no sense. Doesn't he realize the danger? Armando wondered. The smaller two, being toadies, acted how he expected skinheads to act—constantly glancing from side to side as if danger could come from anywhere, giving them the appearance that they might flee at any moment. And they might need to. All it would take is one flare, one single flare to summon the golem, and then it would see they were bigot-tagged and then ...

Armando had a disturbing thought. What if they aren't bigot-tagged? Is that why they dare walk through the city during the day? Is that why they aren't worried someone will summon the golem? Skinheads that aren't bigot-tagged? The idea made his skin crawl.

Reaching into his pocket, Armando pulled out his tagger, a small metal rod like a flashlight. He held it close to his side, trying to be discreet as he flipped it into illumination mode and shone it at the backs of the three skinheads. Two bigot-tags appeared—two, not three. The leader wasn't bigot-tagged.

Armando growled. Now it was clear to him. Of course the toadies were the only ones terrified. They were both marked for death, but their leader? That worthless worm just kept on walking, cocky as an eight-legged dog. He wasn't bigot-tagged, so what did he have to worry about? If the golem was summoned, he could just slip into the crowd and leave his two toadies to their fate.

"What a coward," Armando said. A leader has a duty to his men. A duty! That's why it's best to not be a leader, of course; but if you're stupid enough to be one, then you don't treat your men like that. Skinheads or not, you don't treat your men like that.

Armando's grip tightened on his tagger. I should bigot-tag him, Armando thought. He's too far from here, but I could close the distance in no time. A skinhead walking around in the daytime. A skinhead and a coward too! I should bigot-tag him. I should bigot-tag him and I should shoot up a flare, and then I should stand by and cheer as the golem squeezes him into a bloody pulp.

But, as much as he wanted to, Armando knew he couldn't, so he slid his tagger back into his pocket. He couldn't afford trouble, not now, not with what he had in his pack. I'll make him pay some day, Armando promised himself. I'll make him pay for being such a coward. I'll make him pay for being such a coward on a day I can't afford to make him pay. I'll make him pay doubly for that!

But in the next moment, his anger turned to surprised admiration. A woman was walking past the skinheads, her beautiful painted eyes the only part of her face visible above an elaborate silk veil. And as she walked past them, she turned, extended a slim, shiny tagger, and fired, bigot-tagging the skinhead leader in the back of his neck before turning back in the direction she had been going—the whole act executed in one elegant, fluid motion. The skinhead leader jerked in shock, grabbing his neck where the tagger had struck. He whirled around, a furious look on his face; but the woman had already faded into the crowd. Beautiful execution, Armando thought, simply beautiful.

The skinhead leader, however, didn't share Armando's sentiment. He stood there amidst the moving crowd, rubbing his neck and scanning everyone around him, seeking someone to blame. His eyes locked with Armando's for a moment, forcing Armando to avert his gaze slightly to avoid a challenge, which only caused Armando's anger to flare up even hotter. If any man deserves to be challenged, he thought, then this skinhead coward does. And what could the skinhead do to him? Armando's revolver was safely strapped to his chest. What could the skinhead do to him indeed. But Armando couldn't afford trouble, not now; so he averted his gaze, burning at the necessity, once again promising retribution.

But the fury in the skinhead's face quickly transformed into fear, and he turned around and started to jog up the street, followed closely by his two toadies.

Ha! Armando thought. You're not so cocky anymore, are you, coward? Armando guessed that if he illuminated the sky with his tagger right now, he would see a flare shining brightly above, a flare that was already summoning the golem in this direction.

Ten minutes to his shop. Fifteen minutes before the next patrol. And the skinheads were suddenly running. They darted across the street, almost trampled by a carriage in their haste. Jumping up onto the opposite sidewalk, they sprinted down an alleyway. Where do they think they're going? Armando wondered. There's nothing in that direction, nothing but an old, bombed-out bowling alley.

He worried at what had caused them to take flight. Did they see a patrol? Is that why they're running? But then he heard the giant thuds echoing from the intersection ahead, the ground itself seeming to shake. And a second later he saw the source of the thuds as the golem charged through the intersection. A giant man-shaped creature of hardened clay, the golem cracked the asphalt beneath its feet with each massive step. Everyone scrambled out of its way, for the golem paid no heed to who stood between it and its targets. One horse and rider didn't move fast enough, and the golem mindlessly barreled through them, knocking the horse onto its side and trampling both horse and rider in its pursuit of the bigot-tagged skinheads.

It crashed down the alley, giant footfalls booming back to the street, and only seconds later there was a roar, followed by screams and gunshots. The gunshots were pointless, of course. Bullets went right through the golem's clay, the clay reforming itself immediately after. You couldn't kill the golem, not with a gun.

Armando was already moving again, jogging now in his hurry to escape the scene. "Stupid skinheads," he said. Between the golem and the gunshots, a patrol would be here any minute.

He jogged for two more blocks before slowing to a walk again. Far enough away from the scene now, he didn't want to draw attention to himself, not when he was only minutes away from his shop.

As he entered the market sector, the difference in foot traffic was immediate, masked people spilling off the sidewalks and onto the city streets as they hustled from one errand to another. Armando passed by a group of urchins, their faces brown with dust, tattered clothes exposing thin arms and legs. He pulled out a silver dollar from his pocket and tossed it to them. Armando would never give a handout to an adult. The very idea revolted him. But kids were different. A young girl caught the coin, her hair a rat's nest upon her head. "Thank you, sir!" she said as the other urchins gathered around her excitedly, but Armando was already passing.

He crossed the final street before reaching his own block, the weight of his pack seeming to lighten as it was clear he would not be caught. There was a small crowd gathered at the corner, listening and laughing at a man who stood upon a wooden crate and preached loudly at them. Something about sin, it sounded like. Not a fun gig, Armando thought, feeling a momentary tinge of sympathy for the preacher. The crowd didn't seem very receptive of what he was saying. But Armando had no time for sympathy, and he hurried up the street.

Then he was at his shop. For the dozenth time he reminded himself to repaint his sign. It hung faded and worn above his thick front door. He opened the door and hurried inside, quickly closing it behind himself to keep out as much of the dust as possible. He ripped off his mask and goggles and then grabbed a small battery-operated blow dryer he always kept by the door. The dryer made a high whine as it blew all the dust from his hair, face, and clothes.

"How was the morning?" Armando asked his assistant, Jasper, who had come to gather Armando's dust mask and goggles.

"Slow," Jasper said, returning to the counter and placing the mask and goggles in a bin by the floor.

Armando grunted. A slow morning was bad, but perhaps with Jasper alone in the shop a slow morning was best. Jasper was an honest man, but he was also a coward.

If any trouble had come to the shop while Armando was gone, Jasper wouldn't have been brave enough to do anything about it.

"Put these in the basement," Armando said, handing his pack to Jasper. "Leave them in the pack. I'll sort them later. Be gentle with them."

Jasper nodded. "You got the full shipment, then?"

Armando grunted. "Nearly all. Some were defective."

"And the patrols?"

"They were occupied."

Jasper pulled up the trapdoor behind the counter and descended the stairs into the basement, taking Armando's delivery with him. Armando watched him go, and then he walked up and down the cramped aisles of his small shop, checking the merchandise. He was troubled by the thin layer of dust that had settled over the power aisle, its bins filled with recovered batteries. It was impossible to keep dust from entering the shop on a dust day, but he liked to keep his wares as presentable as possible.

He grabbed a duster and brushed off the batteries. Half of their labels were cracking away, and they didn't look much better with dust off than with dust on, but sometimes it was the little things that made the difference.

Someone was yelling outside. The preacher must have really gotten them riled up this time, Armando thought. What a crummy job, having to constantly remind people of what they weren't supposed to do. It's a lot funner being the one that needs the reminding.

He swapped the duster for a broom and began sweeping up the dust he had knocked unto the ground along with the dust that had followed him into the shop. He swept it into a pile and was about to grab the dustpan when his door flung open and two men burst inside. Armando raised his broom instinctively, holding it like a weapon.

"You can't call that a sin!"

It was the preacher that had run in first, followed by an angry man who was shouting at him. "You can't call that a sin!" the angry man yelled again at the preacher.

"Get out of my shop!" Armando said, advancing on the two of them with broom in hand as if he could sweep them both out. "Get out of my shop!" he repeated.

The angry man turned to him, shaking a finger at the preacher. "He can't preach that!" the angry man said. "He can't call that a sin!"

"Who are you to say what he can and can't call a sin?" Armando said. "And who are you to say it in *my* shop? Get out!" Armando pushed the angry man toward the door.

The angry man stumbled, but when he regained his footing he had a tagger in his hand. Pointing it at the preacher, he fired. The preacher grunted, his head rocking back and hitting the shelf behind him. He grabbed his neck where the bigot-tag had struck.

"What did you just do?" Armando said in disbelief.

"He can't call that a sin!"

"You bigot-tagged him!"

"He can't call that a sin!" the angry man repeated.

"Who cares?" Armando roared. "That's not what the tagger was made for!"

"He can't call that a sin! Everyone knows it! He can't call that a sin! It's not allowed!"

"Who cares what he says is a sin? Who cares what he preached? That's not what the tagger was made for! That's not what the golem was made for! It's meant to handle the skinheads. It's not meant to resolve religious disagreements. He was preaching about sin, not skin! If you don't like his preaching, why don't you get out there and preach yourself?"

The angry man was still pointing his tagger at the preacher, who was rubbing his neck, the preacher's eyes wide in disbelief. Armando struck the angry man's hand with his broom, knocking the tagger to the ground.

"Hey!" the angry man said, grasping his injured hand.

Armando stomped on the tagger, splitting it in two beneath his thick boot.

"Hey!" the angry man repeated. "You broke my tagger!"

"Someone as stupid as you can't be trusted with a tagger," Armando said. He set the head of his broom on the floor and placed both hands on top of the handle, resting his chin above them. "And what am I supposed to do now?" he asked the angry man, who was staring at his broken tagger on the floor. "Now I've got an innocent man in my shop who's been bigot-tagged. What am I supposed to do about that?"

"He's not innocent," the angry man said. "He can't preach that! He's a bigot!"

"He's no bigot. You, however, are an idiot."

"He can't call that a sin!"

Armando pointed the broom at the angry man. "Get out of my shop."

"But—"

"Get out of my shop!" Armando yelled, raising the broom above his head with both hands like a baseball bat and advancing on the angry man. "Get out of my shop!"

The angry man scurried away, running out the door and leaving the shop in silence. Through the window, Armando could see dust swirling around as people walked back and forth along the street, the angry man nowhere to be seen.

"I can't believe he did that," the preacher said.

Armando turned to see the preacher still rubbing his neck. He wondered what it felt like, being bigot-tagged. It's something he had never considered before.

"I was just preaching," the preacher said. "Just preaching against sin, and that man just went off. Shouting at me that I can't preach about that, that I can't even believe that. Then he started shoving me, and he started threatening me. I thought he was going to hit me! So I ran. I ran in here and he bigot-tagged me. He bigot-tagged me! I don't understand it. I was just preaching against sin."

Armando looked back out the window. What kind of a fool would bigot-tag a man for preaching? Was he so insecure about his own beliefs that he had to bring in the golem instead of arguing for himself?

The preacher kept rubbing his neck. "It burns," he said. "Is there any way to take it off?"

"No," Armando said. "Once bigot-tagged, always bigot-tagged."

"But that means the golem ..."

"Yes," Armando said. "That means the golem is going to kill you." He couldn't believe what had happened. An innocent man had just been bigot-tagged. Who would have thought this would ever happen? That's not what taggers were made for. That's not what the golem was made for. And now an innocent man had been bigot-tagged and now an innocent man was going to be killed by the golem. An innocent man in my shop, Armando thought, in *my* shop.

"What am I supposed to do?" the preacher asked.

Armando growled. "Not in my shop," he said.

"What?"

"Not in *my* shop!" Armando walked to the door and flipped his sign to "Closed." He pulled down the blinds on all the windows.

"Here's the plan," Armando said. "We wait here until dark. Chances are the golem won't come down this street. We wait here until dark and then we sneak you out of the city."

"Why is dark any better?"

"The golem can't see very well in the dark. And, more importantly, other people can't see very well in the dark either, so it's less likely a flare will be sent up to summon it."

Armando locked the door. Then he lowered the steel bar across it.

"What are you doing, Armando?"

Armando turned to see Jasper standing behind the counter, his face pale. He must have come up from the basement during the commotion.

"We're closing up early today," Armando told him. "Then I have a night delivery to make to the edge of town."

"What are you doing?" Jasper repeated. "He's been bigot-tagged! We have to give him to the golem!"

"Didn't you see what happened?" Armando asked. "He wasn't supposed to be bigot-tagged."

"But he's been bigot-tagged!" Jasper said. "We have to let the golem kill him!"

"He wasn't supposed to be bigot-tagged. He's an innocent man."

"But he's been bigot-tagged!" Jasper hurried to the door as if he were going to open it.

Armando stood in his way. "Don't you get it?" he said. "Being bigot-tagged doesn't mean anything anymore! Not when someone just whips out their tagger to win an argument."

"But he's been bigot-tagged!"

"Aren't you listening? He wasn't supposed to be! Here," Armando said, pulling his tagger out of his pocket and pointing it at Jasper, only inches from his nose. "How about I bigot-tag you right now? What would you say about that? Would you finally get it then? This isn't what taggers were invented for. They're supposed to be used to bigot-tag the skinheads, not men like the preacher. This wasn't supposed to happen."

Jasper shrunk before the tagger and scurried back behind the counter. "He's been bigot-tagged," Jasper whined. Armando paid him no heed.

"So, that's the plan," Armando said, turning back to the preacher. "Once it's dark, I lead you to the outskirts of town."

"I can't do that," the preacher said.

"What do you mean you can't do that? What part of 'you've been bigot-tagged and the golem is now going to kill you' are you not understanding?"

"I can't just leave," the preacher said. "I have responsibilities here."

"Not anymore."

"You're telling me that I have to be exiled because someone else chose to bigot-tag me?"

"What other choice do you have? I agree it was wrong for him to do. But now what other choice do you have? Do you want my help or not?"

The preacher thought for a moment. "Fine," he relented. "I suppose I could do some good somewhere else. But how long do we have to wait?"

"About six hours—" Armando began before stopping and turning back to the window, listening to the crowd outside. Something was wrong. He leaned one hand upon a small shelf on the wall, the miniature glass figurines upon it rattling briefly, and he opened the blinds with his other hand, peeking out at the street outside.

The glass figurines rattled again.

Armando looked at them. A miniature horse, an elephant, some dogs, a unicorn. He hadn't touched the shelf that time. They bounced up again, the horse and elephant falling to their sides. Armando looked out the blinds. The crowd was fleeing in all directions.

"Downstairs!" Armando yelled, dropping the blinds and running to the preacher. He grabbed the preacher's arm and threw him toward the counter. "The stairs are back there. Downstairs, now!"

"But it can't see—"

"It can sense you if it's close enough. Now move!"

Footsteps were crashing down the street toward the shop. The preacher ran back behind the counter, quickly disappearing below as he fled down the stairs.

Armando turned back toward the windows. He watched the merchandise on his shelves bounce with each giant footstep.

"He's been bigot-tagged," Jasper whined.

"Shut up, you fool," Armando whispered.

The footsteps were closer now, the windows shaking. The glass unicorn fell, shattering into countless pieces as it struck the floor.

Then the footsteps were in front of the shop. And then they were passing it, becoming more and more distant as the golem ran up the street. The rattling ceased. Armando let out a sigh of relief.

But then the footsteps began coming from the other direction.

"What?" Armando said. "Why would it come back?"

"He's been bigot-tagged," Jasper whined again.

"I told you to shut up," Armando said. He rushed to the window and peeked through the blinds. There was no one in sight, just the dust swirling around. The windows were shaking again.

"No," Armando said. "He couldn't have. I smashed his tagger." Yet Armando knew what he would see even before he raised his own tagger in illumination mode and shone it above his shop: a flare shone brightly in the air through the dust.

"That worm!" Armando said. He dropped the blinds and shoved his tagger back in his pocket. "That rotten, little, pathetic tyrant! He shot up a flare somehow! That worm!"

"He's been bigot-tagged!" Jasper said. "We need to give him to the golem."

"How about I give you to the golem, you sniveling coward!" Armando said.

There was a massive crash against the door. Dust flew everywhere as the shelves against the wall all spilled their goods onto the floor. Then another crash. A crack appeared down the middle of the door. The metal bar was bending inward.

"Downstairs!" Armando commanded, running toward the counter.

"We have to give him to—" Jasper began, but Armando grabbed his elbow and hurled him down the steps, Armando right behind. The trapdoor barely closed before the door above burst open. Armando hurried down the stairs and stood next to the preacher. He winced as he listened to the crashes as aisle after aisle was knocked over, metal clanking as it fell, glass breaking, the floor creaking as the golem wandered back and forth.

"I'm sorry," the preacher said, seeing Armando's expression. "Is there anything I can—"

Armando shook his head. "I don't want to even talk about it." More glass broke above. Armando cringed.

"How long before it finds us?" the preacher asked.

Armando shrugged. "I don't think it can find you down here. It can't look down. It can sense you're close, but it can't find you. Not when you're below it."

"So we just wait here until it leaves?"

"No, it will never leave. Not when it's been summoned by a flare. Not when it senses someone near has been bigot-tagged. It won't leave until it kills you."

"So what do we do now?"

Armando looked around the dimly lit basement, bare wood floors and dirt walls, shelves filled with stored goods, support beams standing tall in the dim light. His pack lay by a shelf, its contents once important, now forgotten.

Jasper was muttering to himself, not looking at the two of them.

"Will you shut up?" Armando said.

"He's been bigot-tagged!" Jasper said.

"So what?" Armando said, wanting to throttle the foolish man. "Don't you get it? That doesn't mean anything anymore. Now that the golem is being used to settle disagreements about preaching, what will it be used for next? Where does it stop?"

"But he's been bigot-tagged!"

"He wasn't supposed to be. Don't you get it? That's not what the tagger was made for. That's not what the golem was made for. It's all become corrupted. None of it works anymore."

"But he's been bigot-tagged!"

"Oh, just shut up, you fool! This isn't what taggers were made for!"

Jasper retreated to his muttering and Armando resumed his scanning of the basement. Above, the golem continued wandering in search of the preacher, the floor bending beneath it, the nearest support beam groaning. If that support beam wasn't there, Armando thought, it would fall right on top of us. Then he saw the back door, barely visible behind stacked boxes.

"We'll go out the back," he said, heading toward the door.

The preacher followed after. "But won't the golem sense me leaving and just chase us?"

"Maybe," Armando said, moving the boxes that were blocking the door. "But this leads up to an alley that exits out the other side of the block. Hopefully, he'll get lost."

"Hopefully?"

"Hey, do you have a better idea?" Armando asked, looking back at the preacher.

The preacher shook his head.

"That's what I thought." Armando said. He pulled some keys from his pocket and unlocked the door. Then he opened it. A dark passageway lay beyond. There was a switch by the door, which he flipped, and a light turned on, revealing an iron security gate barring the way.

"Jasper," Armando called to the sulking man, "make yourself useful and grab me the gate key. It's on the shelf by the staircase."

They waited for Jasper to retrieve the key. When he brought it, he wouldn't look at either of them. He just walked over with the key and unlocked the gate.

Armando didn't have time for his foolish assistant. He looked at the preacher. "As soon as we move from below it, the golem is going to follow. Are you ready to run?"

"I think so," the preacher said.

Jasper opened the gate, squeezed through, and flung it shut behind himself, the key in his hand.

"What are you doing?" Armando said. He grabbed the bars and shook the gate. "Open this gate! We need to get out of here!"

"No!" Jasper said, retreating a few steps before turning to face them. "He's been bigot-tagged!" Jasper pointed at the preacher. "He's been bigot-tagged, and the golem has come for him."

"I told you. He wasn't supposed to be," Armando said. "Taggers were invented to bigot-tag the skinheads. If men like the preacher are being bigot-tagged, then being bigot-tagged doesn't mean what it used to mean anymore. It doesn't mean anything anymore."

"But he's been bigot-tagged! He's been bigot-tagged!"

"You idiot!" Armando said. "Can't you think for yourself for a minute? If men who don't deserve to be bigot-tagged are being bigot-tagged, then what does it mean anymore? Here, how do you like this?" Armando pulled out his tagger, pointed it at Jasper's forehead, and fired.

Jasper's head rocked backward, the force of the bigot-tag causing him to stumble back a few feet.

"You just bigot-tagged me!" he said in shock, a hand to his forehead.

"Yes, now do you get it?" Armando asked. "Being bigot-tagged used to mean something. How can it mean anything now if the wrong people are being bigot-tagged?"

"I've been bigot-tagged!" Jasper wailed. He stumbled to the wall and began bashing his head against it. "I've been bigot-tagged!"

"Calm down!" Armando said. "It means nothing! You know you're not a skinhead! It doesn't mean what it used to mean anymore!"

"I've been bigot-tagged!" Jasper wailed again. Then he turned and ran down the passageway, vanishing around a corner.

"You cowardly idiot!" Armando yelled. He cursed and shook the gate futilely. It wouldn't budge.

The preacher was standing beside Armando now, looking down the passageway. "One thing I've learned from all my time preaching," he said, "is that no matter how hard you try to help them, some people simply lack the ability to see anything other than the crude shapes they've learned to base their life around."

"Jasper can't see because Jasper is a fool."

"Yes, and you just ruined his life. He'll never be able to get past being bigot-tagged."

"Yeah, well, he's not my problem anymore. Loyalty runs two ways. He betrayed me. I have no more duty to him."

The preacher stared at Armando for a moment. "But you have a duty to me?"

"The golem's not going to kill an innocent man in my shop."

"I thank you for that, but our options have run out. Perhaps it's time for me to walk up and meet my fate," the preacher said, looking up at the floor above him. The golem was still moving back and forth, dust trickling down from each step as the floorboards strained beneath its weight.

"No," Armando said. "No innocent man is going to be killed by the golem in my shop. It's not right. I won't stand for it."

"Then what will we do? We can't escape out the back way. And you told me the golem will never leave as long as it can sense me near. What will we do? We can't live here forever."

Armando let go of the bars. The preacher was right; there was no way to escape. He walked back to the center of the room and stood beside a support beam. "We'll kill the golem," he said.

The preacher laughed. Then he stopped, seeing Armando's expression. He walked over to stand beside him. "Wait, you're serious, aren't you? I thought the golem couldn't be killed. It's not alive in the first place. How are we supposed to kill it? Bullets do nothing. I've heard that much."

"Bullets do nothing, yes, but ask yourself this: What controls the golem? It's not alive, so how is it that it can see, move, and attack?"

"I have no idea."

"I'll tell you how. It's controlled by a chip, a microprocessor. A chip that's attached in its mouth, directly below its tongue. Remove that chip and the golem comes crashing down."

"If it's that easy, why hasn't a skinhead done it already?"

"Because skinheads are idiots," Armando said. "That, and because its jaw is protected."

"If its jaw is protected, how will we remove the chip?"

Armando looked around the room, searching for something useful. Seeing a shelf full of metal goods, he walked over and began rummaging through the items. Then he pulled out what he had been looking for—fireplace tongs. "We'll use this to pull it out of its mouth," he said, walking back to the center of the room.

"Okay, but how do we get to it? You said the jaw was protected."

"Haven't you ever seen the golem attack?"

"No."

"It always roars at its prey. Once it opens its mouth, I'll grab the chip with the tongs and pull it out."

The preacher considered this for a moment. "I take it I'm supposed to be the bait?"

"That's the plan."

"So we walk up through the trapdoor and somehow you pull the chip out before the golem crushes the life out of me?"

"No, it might rush us before we both have a chance to get up through the trapdoor. We need to bring it down here."

"How are you going to do that? It won't even fit through the trapdoor, and it would crush the stairs."

Armando leaned against the support beam and tapped it with the tongs. "We'll bring the golem down to us."

The preacher grunted in surprise. "But that will destroy your shop," he said.

Armando held up a hand, suppressing further discussion. "I told you. We're not going to talk about that. Besides, it's too late now. Anyway, here is the plan. Once the golem is directly above us, I kick out the support beam and we let it fall down into the basement. You hide there on the other side of the room. The fall should confuse the golem for a moment, but then it'll see you and open its mouth to roar, and I'll be there with the tongs ready to pull out the chip."

"You make it sound so easy. But you're forgetting one thing."

"What's that?"

"Say your plan works. Say we pull out the chip and destroy it, killing the golem. What happens then? What about the skinheads?"

"If we don't kill it, it will go on killing innocents."

"I'm just one man. Wouldn't it be worth it for society to sacrifice just one man?"

"No, that's just the start. You were bigot-tagged today for your preaching, but what will we be bigot-tagged for tomorrow? Because of our politics? Because of what food we eat or what music we listen to? Because of what entertainment we watch? The golem was never meant to be used for settling disagreements, but now that it's been used for one, it can just as easily be used for another. We have no choice. We have to destroy it."

"And the skinheads?"

"The skinheads are idiots and they are weak. We don't need the golem to take care of them for us anymore. We can handle them ourselves."

The preacher scratched at his neck where he had been bigot-tagged. "I see your point," he said. Then he sighed. "Well, let's get this over with. I can't say I like the idea of being bait, but I also don't like the idea of being stuck down here forever."

Armando nodded. "Alright," he said. "You go stand back by that far wall over there."

The preacher obeyed, hurrying across the room and pressing himself against the wall, a nervous look on his face. Then they waited, both of them staring at the floorboards above as the golem continued its slow wandering, the groaning of the wood announcing its location to them below.

Armando waited until the groaning was directly overhead, then he kicked the support beam. His first kick did nothing, but the second shifted the beam slightly. The golem was walking away now. Armando knew he had little time before it would be too far. Lowering his head, he charged at the support beam, striking it with his entire force. It gave way and his momentum carried him forward, Armando falling down, the support beam on top of him, as the floor above collapsed and a giant shape dropped down from above.

The ground shook. Dust and debris filled the air. Armando coughed and pushed the support beam off himself. He rose to his knees, looking for the tongs he had dropped when the floor came down. A large shape rose beside him. Armando looked up at it. He had never seen the golem so close. It seemed so thick, so solid. Silently, the golem bent over and picked up a massive leg that must have broken off in the fall. It held the separated leg against its hip, and Armando watched as the clay began to knit together, clay reattaching to clay. Then he saw the tongs on the ground behind the golem. He scrambled to them and picked them up in the same moment that the golem noticed the preacher. Opening its mouth, it roared, the sound bouncing around the basement and ringing in Armando's ears. Armando darted forward, trying to reach inside its mouth with the tongs, but he was a second too late and he struck jaw instead. Then the golem was moving, striding toward the preacher with heavy steps, crushing the debris below it.

"Hey!" Armando said, trying to distract it. But the golem ignored him, its full concentration on the preacher, who stood pale against the wall. It knocked over shelves as it continued walking toward him.

"Hey!" Armando yelled, and he threw the tongs at the golem's back to no effect. Then he drew out his revolver and shot it. "Hey!" he yelled again.

The golem had almost reached the preacher. Only one shelf blocked the way. The golem knocked it over easily, crushing the contents as it continued forward.

"Save yourself," the preacher said to Armando.

"No!" Armando said. He fired another bullet at the golem.

"You tried," the preacher said. "You tried and it was noble and I thank you for it. Now just save yourself." Then he closed his eyes and bowed his head, resigned to his fate as the golem grasped him in two massive hands and lifted him into the air.

"Not in my shop!" Armando said.

"There's nothing you can do," the preacher grunted, his face turning red as the golem began to crush him.

But there was something Armando could do. He pulled out his tagger and aimed it at his face. Then he pulled the trigger and bigot-tagged himself in the cheek, his head rocking to the side slightly from the impact.

It felt wrong. He shouldn't have been bigot-tagged and it felt wrong, but he had no time for that now. "Hey!" he yelled at the golem, waving his hands to catch its attention.

The preacher was moaning in its grip. "Hey!" Armando yelled again. But the golem ignored him, intent only on killing the bigot-tagged preacher.

"Hey!" Armando yelled one last time. Then he lifted his tagger above his head and fired off a flare, and the basement filled with invisible heat. The golem dropped the preacher, confused at the mixed signals. It turned and Armando looked into its thoughtless eyes. Then he saw them change, a targeting when the golem realized Armando was bigot-tagged. Opening its mouth, the golem roared at him, and suddenly Armando realized he had no plan. He backed away as the golem rushed toward him, Armando firing useless bullet after useless bullet. He aimed for the mouth, hoping to somehow strike the chip, but the bullets did nothing, and then the golem had reached him, its hands tight around his sides, its blank eyes staring into his face. It started to squeeze. Armando felt his ribs begin to crack. It was all so wrong. This wasn't what the golem had been meant to do. It was only supposed to be used against the racist skinheads. It had never been meant to attack innocent people simply because someone had bigot-tagged them. It was all so wrong. This wasn't how it was supposed to be.

Breathing became impossible and the pain unbearable, darkness closing in around him. Someone was yelling, something hitting the golem on the side of the head. Fireplace tongs? The golem turned and roared, and in the middle of the darkness Armando saw a dull piece of metal below its tongue. His strength nearly spent, he darted his hand forward and grasped the metal chip, yanking it out of the golem's mouth…

He groaned when the ground hit him, his breath knocked out of him, his ribs pure agony. Slowly, he turned onto his back and stared at the ceiling above. Light shone through the hole the golem had made in its fall.

"Are you alright?" the preacher was saying. Armando looked over at the golem that stood above him, its arms still outstretched, its face locked looking in the other direction. He sat up and coughed into his knees, the coughing causing a sharp pain in his sides, which made him fall over again. The preacher grabbed his hand and helped him rise onto one foot and then the other.

"We did it," the preacher said, supporting Armando in front of the inert golem.

"Not quite," Armando whispered. He held the chip up for the preacher to see, just a plain chunk of metal, all its secrets buried deep inside. Then he dropped it to the ground and stomped on it, crushing it. As soon as he did so, the golem broke apart, chunks of clay coming unknit and spilling on the ground all around them.

A clay hand tumbled to rest atop the preacher's foot. Armando kicked it away and the hand disintegrated into small clumps. "Not in my shop," Armando said, but his talking caused another sharp pain in his sides. He gritted his teeth and closed his eyes.

When he opened them, he saw his tagger lying on the floor, its shiny metal standing out amidst the crumbling clay. Armando stared at the tagger, feeling the wrongness of the undeserved bigot-tag he had been marked with.

He smashed the tagger beneath his boot.

The Planner's Utopia

THE CARDINAL SOARED ALONG THE CEILING of the warehouse, red feathers flashing beneath fluorescent light after fluorescent light, the bird's energy so strange in that silent space. It twisted around perfectly positioned air vents as it flew above precisely aligned gurneys, row upon row of which filled the warehouse; but the cardinal did not notice such things as it flew from one end of the warehouse to the other and back again. It flew because it could. It flew because it wanted to. Such movement. Such beauty. Such freedom.

Its red wings tilted, and the cardinal glided down to rest upon a gurney in the center of the room. Gingerly, it crept forward on the coarse, gray sheet, its small searching eyes examining the shadow below the bald head of the human lying there, the human silent and unmoving. The cardinal had hoped to find food, but there was none; and so the cardinal spread its wings and took to the air again, landing on a gurney a row over, where another silent human lay. But there was no food there either, nothing but a softly breathing human and coarse, gray sheets. The cardinal spread its wings once more, flew, and landed on another gurney, then another, and another, all of them containing a silent human, none of them containing food. The warehouse was perfectly still, perfectly sterile.

The cardinal took to the air again and flew from side to side, searching the ground below it. There! Something next to the wall. Something different. The cardinal swooped down and landed a few feet away. It cocked its head to one side and eyed what lay upon the floor. Then, recognizing the breadcrumbs for the food they were, it bounced forward and grabbed a crumb in its small beak.

A shadow passed above the cardinal, followed by a thud on all sides and then darkness. The cardinal spread its wings to fly but hit something hard right above it. It tried again, only to be blocked once more. Then it stopped, subdued, and waited in the darkness, a darkness that seemed to drag on forever until finally a crack of light appeared on the floor. The crack grew bigger, and a hand reached in and grasped the cardinal, a hand belonging to the planner, who picked the red bird up from underneath the makeshift trap and held it out in front of him.

The bird was really quite beautiful, the planner thought. He hadn't seen such a vibrant red in years, so different from the grays and browns he was accustomed to in his little slice of paradise.

Imprisoned in the planner's hand, the bird looked at the planner with eyes uncertain yet empty of fear. It seemed … curious. Then it chirped at him. A lovely little sound, which reminded the planner of his youth. He remembered sitting outside beneath the trees in the times before. The bird chirped again. So lovely, the planner thought. He wondered how many citizens could hear it. Citizen #50 and citizen #60 were closest. Certainly they were close enough to hear it, but few others could, which was a pity. If only everyone were able to hear it equally, then it could remain. If only. But like so many things in nature, that was impossible. The bird chirped once more, the beautiful notes stirring something within the planner. But what must be done must be done. He sighed with regret. Then he grasped the bird's head with his other hand and twisted, snapping its neck.

Silence. Equal silence.

A thrill of satisfaction filled the planner, the same thrill that always came when his actions brought equality. And yet in his mind lingered those two words: if only. He sighed again as he looked at the dead bird in his hand. Such beauty. Such wild, unpredictable beauty. A wild creature could never be allowed inside the warehouse, of course. He knew that, and yet he still felt regret.

If only.

Such a beautiful bird it had been, so full of life, of energy. Its chirping so sweet, so lovely. If only, if only, but no. Its song could never fill the warehouse. Some citizens might hear it, but many would not, and that wouldn't be fair. That wouldn't be equal. And, therefore, that couldn't be permitted.

Everyone must be equal, the planner reminded himself. It's better for all to have none than for some to have more.

He started toward the utility room to dispose of the dead bird. His feet were padded to mute any noise, and yet he still walked as gently as possible to ensure no citizens could hear him passing. That was as it should be. Why should some citizens get to hear him when others could not? Equal. Perfect. Just as it should be. The bird had not been as it should be. The bird had been wild. It had been unpredictable. It had been uncontrollable. It had been unequal. It had been free. He couldn't allow a wild creature like that inside the warehouse. Wild creatures—free creatures—are the spawn of nature, and nature doesn't respect equality. All of the planner's efforts, all of his work, nature would throw it all away in a moment if the planner let his guard down. How long had the front door been open? Only a minute or two. Just long enough for him to carry the supplies inside. Only a minute or two, but long enough for the bird to fly in, long enough for nature to once again try to destroy the equality he had so carefully cultivated. He had to be diligent. He had to be dependable. The citizens were counting on him, all 116 of them. He was the only thing that stood between them and the ravages of inequality.

Once inside the utility room, the planner opened the small chute to the incinerator. He dropped the dead bird inside and shut the chute. He would have equality. They all would have it. Equality, blessed equality, not the unfair barbarism of nature. He pressed a button and heard the soft whoosh as the incinerator fired up. Nature could try again and again to destroy his perfectly created equality, but he would always be there to stop it. He would always be there to clean up nature's mess.

He stepped softly back into the warehouse and looked out at the room full of perfectly equal citizens, feeling once again the thrill of satisfaction. How content the citizens must feel, he thought, all of them lying there on their gurneys together, everything perfect, everything equal, nothing to differentiate one from another. Silent, unmoving, equal. It was utopia. It was paradise. And it was all because of him. He was the planner. He made it all possible.

The planner stood there silently, admiring his handiwork, reveling in the satisfaction that was his due. Then, with a flicker, a light on the other side of the warehouse went out, and the planner's satisfaction vanished as the suddenly dim area marred the perfectly arranged lighting of the room. Panic exploded in his gut. Inequality! He rushed forward, so disturbed that he forgot to tread softly; and in his haste his foot caught on one of the citizen's IV stands, tripping the planner and almost toppling the IV stand as he fell over.

Calm down, he told himself as he lifted himself up off the floor. You'll only make things worse if you rush. It can wait a moment. Don't upset things more by rushing around. But his guilt spoke to him, as it so often did. It screamed and thrashed inside his mind. *Inequality! Inequality! Inequality! Inequality!*

Forcing himself to move slowly, the planner scooted the IV stand back to its proper place. Then he lifted the gray sheet away from citizen #92 to examine the citizen's arm. The IV tube hadn't come all the way out, thank goodness, but the tape had been pulled from the citizen's skin, causing a visible abrasion. The planner examined the damage. Well, I'm going to have to settle that, he thought, and he looked around the room at all the citizens in their beds, all 116 of them. He sighed, imagining the work he had ahead of him. But everyone must be equal.

The planner took a small tape measure out of his pocket and measured the size of the abrasion. *You'll never get it exactly right,* his guilt told him. But he had to do his best. The citizens were counting on him. He had to do his best. Everyone must be equal.

He memorized the measurement, placed the tape measure back in his pocket, and returned the citizen's sheet to its proper place. Then, slowly and carefully, he walked toward the site of inequality, which was between citizen #23 and citizen #24. He examined the light fixture above, where one of the fluorescent tubes had gone out and left the two citizens in a slightly dimmer light than the rest. Not a horrible difference, but a difference still the same, and a difference simply wouldn't do.

At least it's an easy fix, the planner told himself. He returned to the utility room and retrieved the ladder. Then, carefully navigating between the IV stands and gurneys, he brought it to the site of the inequality, where he left it standing as he went to gather a replacement tube from the supply room.

The supply room was a small entrance room at the front of the warehouse. In times before, this had likely been a reception area, or perhaps a break room. Now he used it to store their supplies. The robot couriers left the deliveries outside the front door, so it made sense to keep the supplies here. That way he wouldn't have to carry them across the warehouse floor and risk disturbing the perfect equality of the citizens.

He searched through the boxes for the spare light tubes, passing over boxes full of medication, nutrients, spare sheets, catheters, towels, razor blades. Then he found it, a large narrow box labeled "fluorescent tubes." He set it on the ground and opened it.

It was empty.

Panic exploded once more in the planner's gut. This was supposed to be an easy fix! He turned the box upside down and shook it. Empty. Empty. Empty. His guilt roused inside of him. No, there must be a spare tube somewhere, he told himself. He hurried over to the unstacked boxes, today's shipment, which he hadn't had time to stack yet because the bird had flown in while he was carrying the boxes inside. Frantically, he tore through them. No fluorescent tubes. Why hadn't he ordered replacements?

And his guilt scolded him. *Inequality! What are you going to do about the inequality?*

The warehouse wasn't equal. His paradise had been marred. In desperation, the planner unlocked the front door and looked outside, hoping he had left a box behind in his earlier haste; but there was nothing there, nothing but overgrown vegetation in what had once been a parking lot.

Back inside, he looked through the stacked boxes once more, his hands beginning to twitch.

Inequality! Inequality! Inequality! His guilt was screaming at him.

It's not so bad, he lied to himself. It's not such a big difference. He returned to the warehouse to get another look, hoping to be convinced of his lie. He saw the ladder, and there, between citizen #23 and citizen #24, it was noticeably dimmer.

The planner shook his head. We'll just have to wait, he told himself. He returned to the utility room and logged onto the terminal to request new light tubes. It would be two weeks before the next shipment arrived.

Two weeks! his guilt screamed. *How could you let this happen?*

It's not so bad, the planner told himself. Citizen #23 and citizen #24 still have light. Not quite as much as the rest, but it's not so bad.

You call this equality? You are no better than those before. It's your fault. The citizens are unequal and it's all your fault!

But there's nothing I can do, he reasoned with his guilt. He had no spare light tubes, and the robot couriers wouldn't return for two more weeks. They wouldn't come back before it was his turn. That wouldn't be fair. There were many warehouses to deliver to, many planners to supply.

But what will you do about the inequality?

We'll just have to wait. It's not so bad.

That's a lie! Inequality! Inequality! Inequality!

It's not so bad. It's just a little dimmer. The citizens' eyes are all closed anyway. They probably don't even notice the difference.

You are no better than those before. Justifications! Reasons! Excuses! You are no better than those before. The citizens are unequal! Look at you, lounging around in your pampered, privileged state. The citizens are unequal and you don't even care!

Yes, I care, the planner argued with his guilt. I care. I care about equality. I care about everyone having the same.

But his guilt wasn't listening. *Inequality! Inequality! Inequality!* it screamed in his mind. *Inequality! Inequality! Inequality!*

The planner shook with anxiety. How could he have let this happen? His paradise, his utopia—gone, all gone. How could he have let this happen? I do care, he whimpered. I do care.

Then do something, he told himself. Prove that you care.

But there are no spare light tubes, he said to himself. There is nothing I can do.

Yes, there is. There's more inequality here than just from light.

And then he remembered the abrasion. How could he have forgotten? That was something he could fix. That was something he could make equal!

He hurried back into the warehouse and began his work. It was tricky. He had to rip the tape off each arm in just the right way to give the same size of abrasion. He had to be cautious. If he ripped too much and gave too large of an abrasion, then he would have to go back through all the citizens again.

Everyone must be equal.

It was easier to make a small abrasion first, and then reset the tape and do it again and again until bit by bit it had reached the equal size.

But the color is not the same, his guilt told him. *Some abrasions are darker than others. This isn't equality. You are fooling yourself. Some have more than others. This isn't equality.*

It's the right measurement, the planner insisted. I'm giving everyone else the same size abrasion. It's the right measurement. It's equal. Everyone is equal. Everyone is the same.

Except they weren't the same, and he knew it. The color of the abrasions really weren't equal. But that would be impossible! he insisted to himself. He had to focus on the possible. He had to focus on what he could do. But his guilt was right, his guilt was right, his guilt was right—no, he had to focus on the possible. The planner shook the doubts from his mind. He was making the citizens equal. He was. He was making them equal.

And so he went from citizen to citizen, from row to row, working late into the night until he was done. But the thrill of satisfaction at bringing equality did not come to him. He had been so intent on giving everyone the same size abrasion he had almost forgotten the inequality of the lights. But now, realizing he had almost forgotten, he remembered.

You are no better than those before! his guilt reminded him. *You let the inequality persist! You let the inequality persist and you do nothing!*

There is nothing I can do. I have to wait for new light tubes. There is nothing I can do!

You are no better than those before!

No, I am a planner! I seek social justice! I seek equality!

This is not equality. Some have more than others. This is not equality.

He was exhausted, and there was nothing he could do. Exhausted, so exhausted that he had already started walking back to the utility room to sleep before he realized he had almost forgotten his nightly routine. It was essential that he check the medication levels of all the citizens before he went to bed. If any of them ran out of medication while he was sleeping...

Thankfully, no refills were necessary. They would all last until morning. And so, the planner trudged his way back into the utility room, where he pulled the cot down from the wall, lay down, and tried to sleep.

But sleep would not come to him. Not in the midst of so great a failure.

You are no better than those before!

No, I seek social justice! I seek equality!

You are no better than those before. Some have more and you permit it. You are no better than those before!

His breathing became shallow, and he began to rock back and forth on his cot. I can't give more to those who have less. There is no more to give!

Some have more. That is inequality. That is the very definition of inequality.

But I have no more to give...

Then the planner sprang out of bed. The solution was so simple! Why hadn't he thought of it before? He couldn't give more to those who had less, but he could take away from those who had more!

His exhaustion erased by excitement, the planner grabbed the ladder and got to work, removing light tube after light tube until every fixture in the entire warehouse had only a single tube. Then, standing on the outskirts of the warehouse floor, he looked out over his dim perfection, and satisfaction filled him once more. It might be hard to see the far end of the room now, but it was equal. He had done it.

It's better for all to have none than for some to have more, he said to himself. Everyone must be equal.

Yes, he was a planner. Because of him—social justice was possible. Because of him—equality was possible. He was a planner, and today he had defeated one more type of inequality. Once more nature had tried to mar perfection, but he had prevailed against it! He had prevailed, and the citizens were equal once more. Equal once more!

Even his guilt seemed to agree. It was silent as he lay down on his cot; and soon, filled with satisfaction, he fell asleep.

The next morning he was as busy as ever. All of the medications had to be refilled, which was a time-consuming process. This was followed by the necessary airflow and temperature measurements to ensure that nothing had gone awry. The ventilation system had taken months of painstaking work to get right.

And you had tried to take a shortcut! his guilt accused him. *You had tried to move the gurneys instead of the vents, ignoring the blatant inequality of the space between the cots!*

Yes, but I solved it, the planner replied. Now I just need to keep it solved.

Thankfully, the airflows and temperatures were still perfectly equal, and he was able to move on to the next part of his morning routine: shaving each citizen's head. He hadn't always shaved every head. Initially, he had thought that only the males needed shaving. How foolish he had been! It wasn't until he rescued citizen #56, an old female, that he realized his error. As he had prepped the new citizen for her stay in paradise, he had noticed the bald spot atop her head. What a fool he had been! He had never even considered that hair inequality extended to females, but of course it did—females can go bald as well!

He had found a new source of inequality, something that he had never imagined was a problem before but that now needed to be dealt with decisively. And so, from that day forward, he shaved every head, male and female. The process took twice as long as before. But equality cannot be rushed.

You are no better than those before! Excuses! Justifications!

The planner ignored his guilt at past mistakes. He reminded himself how he had solved the light inequality the night before, the dimness of the room a testament of his success. And the memory brought the satisfaction back, a satisfaction so sweet that he started humming to himself. Not out loud of course—it wouldn't be fair for some citizens to hear his tune while others could not.

He sat on a small stool as he shaved each citizen, moving from one gurney to the next, humming happily in his head as he carefully cut every hair, not leaving even a trace of stubble. Perfection. Equality.

"Hello?"

The planner froze. Had there been a noise? He looked around the room. It was harder to see now with the light so dim.

"Hello?"

The planner dropped his razor. Had that been a human voice? A human voice?

Nature is always trying to destroy equality!

The planner stood and looked around the room. There was no one there.

"Hello?"

The voice was closer this time. It's coming from the supply room, the planner realized. He padded softly in that direction. Someone had broken in! How could they … oh, no!

He remembered the afternoon before. He remembered his panic and his rush. Had he locked the front door after checking for fluorescent tubes outside? No, he hadn't. He hadn't locked it, and now someone had come inside. They threatened everything.

How could you let this happen?

He had to stop them. The citizens were counting on him. He had to stop them before they disturbed the citizens …

But it was too late. Before the planner could reach the door, a woman walked into the warehouse. Clad in a mixture of cotton and leather, she had a bow and quiver slung over one shoulder and a pack upon her back. Long red hair fell down around her shoulders, and a large metal trap hung from her pack on one side.

"Hello?" the woman said as she entered the warehouse. Then she stopped, eyes wide.

The planner dropped to his knees and hid behind a gurney. What was he supposed to do now?

She will ruin everything!

The woman walked forward, slowly approaching the nearest gurney. She stood and looked at the citizen who lay there. Then she pulled their sheet down a few inches. The planner trembled at the unbalance she was creating.

Stop her! Stop her! She will ruin everything!

She pulled the sheet back up. But not to the right spot. *Inequality! Inequality! Inequality!*

The woman laid her hand on the citizen's forehead as if feeling for a temperature, and the planner could take the inequality no more. He leapt to his feet and ran toward her. Stop! he tried to whisper. But it had been so long since he had last spoken, his mouth couldn't form the words. "Stop!" his lips finally managed.

The woman jumped back, one hand reaching instinctively for her bow, but she relaxed when she saw him.

"Oh!" she said, her voice loud enough for an entire section of citizens to hear.

But not the rest! Not the rest!

"I was looking for water," the woman said as the planner reached her, "and the door was unlocked and I, I ..." Then she stopped and her hands snapped formally to her sides as she gave a slight bow. "I am called Anaya," she said, and she stood there, hands tight at her sides, head slightly bowed, as if expecting some action from the planner; but he ignored her, focusing instead on the citizen's sheet. Just as I feared, he said to himself. She didn't set it correctly.

"What's wrong with them?" Anaya asked, dropping her formal stance and moving to stand beside the planner.

"They are sick," the planner whispered.

"What? I'm sorry, but you need to speak louder. I can't hear you."

The planner turned to face her, willing as much volume out of his voice as possible. "They are sick!"

"Oh," Anaya said. Pity entered her face as she looked down at the citizen once more. "Will they ever get better?"

"They are better now," the planner told her.

"Now?" Anaya asked. She tried to guess at his meaning. "Oh, you're saying that they'll never get better, that they'll always be like this." She rested her hand on the citizen's forehead again, her eyes full of pity.

"Stop that!" the planner snapped at her.

Anaya yanked her hand away. "What? What did I do?" Her eyes grew wide. "Are they contagious?" She took a step back.

"Of course they are," the planner told her. "They are humans!" He stared at the citizen's forehead for a moment. *Inequality! Inequality!*

"You must touch all their foreheads now," the planner said. "You touched one. Now you must touch them all."

"What?" Anaya said. She took another step back. "But you just said they're contagious! I'm not going to touch any of them!"

"But you must," the planner insisted. "Otherwise, it wouldn't be equal." He returned his attention to the sheet, pulling carefully to align it with the markings on each side of the gurney. Then, the sheets equal once more, he felt the familiar satisfaction fill him, allowing him to forget for a moment the inequality her forehead touching had created.

Anaya brushed a strand of red hair out of her face. "How many are here?" she asked the planner.

"116," the planner whispered, eyes still on the sheet, double-checking that he had in fact gotten it right.

"116?" Anaya said. "And you care for them all by yourself?"

"Yes," the planner whispered. "I keep them equal."

Anaya whistled as she looked around the room. "That's a lot of work for one person."

Inequality! Inequality!

The planner whirled toward her. "Stop doing that!" he hissed.

"What?" Anaya asked, confusion on her face. She brushed another red hair away. Her hair seemed to have a mind of its own, so wild, so unpredictable. "I was just saying that that's a lot of work for one person. Maybe you should get some help."

They would ruin everything! They would ruin everything!

"No, no, no, no, no, no, no," the planner said, trembling slightly at the thought. Equality was so precise, so difficult. But that was something he could never explain, so he didn't even try.

Anaya shifted her pack, the large metal trap jingling with the movement. The planner eyed the trap, and then he looked back at Anaya, who seemed to notice the IVs for the first time. Reaching up, she took the bag of medication and examined it, but the bag was blank. All she could see was the clear liquid inside.

"Does the medication help them?" Anaya asked.

"Yes," the planner said. "It keeps the sickness away. It keeps them equal."

"Equal?" Anaya looked around at the rows of motionless bodies.

"Yes, equal. They are all equal here." Satisfaction swelled within the planner. He stood proudly. "This is utopia. They are all equal here."

"Utopia?" Anaya laughed at what she thought was a joke.

But the planner did not laugh. He just looked at her, one of his eyes slightly twitching.

"I'm sorry," Anaya said. "I know you work hard, and I can't even imagine how exhausting it must be to care for so many sick people, but this is no utopia. It's clean. I'll give you that. But I'd take the outside world anytime. Just the silence is enough to drive one batty."

Silence. Blessed silence. At the mention of the word, the planner realized the gross inequality of sound he was permitting. It was so difficult to regulate sound. Like so many things in nature, it resisted the very idea of equality. Perhaps with a complex system of precisely tuned microphones and speakers—but no, that would be too difficult. Silence would have to do. It's better for all to have none than for some to have more.

"The water is in the utility room," the planner whispered to Anaya, and he motioned for her to follow him.

As they walked, he thought of what she had told him, about how she preferred the outside world to his utopia here inside. How could she not see? How could she not understand? This was utopia. This was perfection.

"Things have never been better than they are now," the planner whispered. He gestured toward the citizens. "Look at them. Has there ever been such equality in all the world? No. In times before, inequality was everywhere. Income inequality . . . all kinds of inequality . . . everywhere, absolutely everywhere!"

Anaya looked at the rows of inert bodies and imagined their muscles atrophying into nothing. Was that even life? Why had they even been born? A shallow grave seemed more meaningful than this. At least then your body would give nutrients back into the earth, which would become flowers, trees, and animals. But this, this was a horror show. She wouldn't say that to the strange caretaker, of course. That would only hurt his feelings. Besides, he seemed a little mixed up. All this talk about equality like it was the only thing that mattered. And why was the light in here so dim?

"Equality," the planner continued with his whispering. "Equality is the goal. Equality is everything."

Anaya stopped and faced him. "Have you ever wondered if maybe you're focusing on the wrong goal?"

The planner's eyes narrowed in confusion. "What could be greater than equality?"

"How about freedom?"

"Freedom?" the planner scoffed. "Freedom always ruins the perfection of equality."

Anaya shook her head. "Equality is a noble goal," she said, "but freedom must be its foundation. Freedom is greater than equality. If you have freedom without equality, you can use that freedom to achieve the goal of equality. But if you have equality without freedom, you have nothing and you can do nothing. All you have is a sterile hell. Equal? Sure. Equal in nothingness."

She looked out over the silent humans lying upon the gurneys, and a chill ran down her spine. Imagine lying there, wasting away in perfect equality.

The planner scowled at Anaya. She didn't understand. Equality was the greatest good and therefore freedom must be the greatest evil. But there was no use discussing it any further. He motioned again for her to follow him, and they continued through the warehouse in silence until they came to the door to the utility room.

"You can leave your pack out here," he told her. "There is a faucet inside. Take as much water as you wish." He opened the door for her and stood there waiting patiently.

Anaya shrugged her pack onto the ground, but she kept the bow and quiver on her back. She pulled a large canteen from her pack and then walked through the door into the utility room.

"Thank you," she told him as she looked around the sparse room. The faucet was on the far wall along with an old terminal. On the wall next to it was a stack of flattened boxes and what appeared to be an incinerator chute. A simple metal cot was attached to the other wall.

"I have something I must attend to," the planner told her, and the door closed, leaving Anaya alone in the utility room.

What a strange man, she thought. Then she reminded herself how hard it must be to care for so many sick people. 116? What an incredible burden.

She turned on the faucet and stuck her face under the water to drink a few gulps. It was cool and clean. She filled her canteen to the top, and then she took a few more gulps before shutting off the faucet.

This whole place was disturbing. All these sick people, all this silence. And the caretaker, what a strange man. Such weird ideas he had. The solitude must be driving him mad. She wanted nothing more than to gather her pack and get out of this place as soon as possible; yet, seeing the stack of flattened boxes, she couldn't help feeling a little curious. She examined the labels. Most of them seemed to be food, some sort of processed material, apparently provided via IV. There were a lot of medication boxes as well. The medication's name was unfamiliar, but there was a description below in tiny letters. She picked up a box and studied it closely. Most of the language was medical jargon, but one word caught her eye: "Sedative."

Anaya dropped the box and grabbed her bow, an arrow nocked before she even turned around. Now it was clear to her. All those rows of motionless people—of sleeping people. He had told her they were sick. He had told her the medication made them better. Now Anaya knew what sickness he was curing with his medication.

She pushed open the door slowly, her bow drawn tight, an arrow ready to be loosed. Entering the warehouse, she looked out across the prisoners, squinting in the dim light for a sight of their captor. She stepped sideways, her back to the wall, an arrow trained toward the room. She would kill this misguided tyrant, and then she would free his prisoners, and then—

Her left leg exploded in pain as metal spikes drove through her skin, shattering the bone. She screamed and fell to the ground, dropping her bow and grasping the trap that had caught her leg. Her own trap! She pulled at it, but it wouldn't come loose. The pain was unbearable. Something was held over her mouth and then . . .

➤   ◀

The planner opened the incinerator chute and dropped the last handful of red hair inside. Such a pity, he thought as the fire consumed it. Such lovely hair. If only everyone had been born with such hair, then they could keep it.

If only.

But they hadn't. Few were blessed with such beauty, and what about the rest? How would that be fair? How would that be equal? If only, if only, but no.

He returned to the gurney of citizen #117 in the warehouse. She looked so different lying there, her head shaved, her eyes closed, her breathing soft. And seeing her lying there in the silence of equality, the planner couldn't help but feel a little bit of loss. He had seen her walking. He had heard her talking. It was a pity that things had to be this way—yet this was how they had to be. Nature is inherently unequal. Some people are stronger. Some people are faster. Some people are smarter. Some people work harder. You can't have that and have all results be equal. The solution, then, is to not have that at all.

It's better for all to have none than for some to have more, the planner said to himself.

Yes, citizen #117 looked very different from before. She looked equal. And the planner felt that familiar thrill of satisfaction. He had done well. The barbarism of nature had been pushed back, and the world had become a little bit more equal. In times before, inequality had been everywhere, but it was a new day now, a new age. And he was part of it. He was part of it and inequality was gone. All of the citizens were perfectly equal.

The planner raised citizen #117's sheet to examine where her left foot had been. That had been very unfortunate. He had tried and tried, but in the end had been unable to save it. He took out his tape measure and measured how much had been cut off.

Now he had much work to do, much, much work; but satisfaction still swelled inside him, telling him it was all worth it. He hummed a happy tune in his head as he returned the new citizen's sheet to its proper place, aligning it perfectly on the gurney. Then he stood and carried his medical bag to the next citizen. Pulling the sheet up, he exposed the left leg of citizen #116, measured the necessary length, and marked it precisely on the citizen's leg. Then he reached into his medical bag and pulled out a saw. He placed the saw carefully on the measured mark and began to cut, red blood pouring down on the coarse, gray sheet.

Everyone must be equal.

Dandelion Seeds

THERE WAS ONCE A BEAUTIFUL BACKYARD with thick green grass from side to side, everywhere except for one small section of the yard known as the dandelion patch, where dandelions bloomed in all their splendor.

One day, the dog of the home decided it wanted a snack. Unable to find any dog treats, it rummaged through the gardener's tools instead, finding a bag of dandelion seeds, which it promptly tore apart in the backyard, leaving remnants of plastic throughout the yard and dandelion seeds absolutely everywhere.

When the gardener discovered what the dog had done, he was distressed. Now dandelions were going to bloom all over the yard. He was going to lose his job!

One of the garden gnomes observed the fretting gardener. "Don't worry," the garden gnome told the gardener. "Those are dandelion seeds. They never grow in the grass. They only grow in a dandelion patch. Everyone knows that."

"Are you sure?" the gardener asked.

"Oh, definitely. Dandelion seeds growing in the grass? That's absurd."

"Well, that's a relief," the gardener said, and he promptly forgot all about it.

But two months later, the yard was covered with dandelions.

The gardener looked out at the once beautiful grass in despair. "How could this happen?" he asked the garden gnome. "You told me dandelion seeds wouldn't grow in the grass!"

The garden gnome, being a garden gnome, didn't remember the earlier conversation. "They're seeds," he told the gardener. "What did you expect was going to happen? Did you think dandelions are magically confined to only a small section of the yard? Where did you get a silly idea like that?"

"Where did I get a silly idea like that?" The gardener raised his hands in exasperation. "That's what you told me! You told me not to worry! You told me dandelion seeds would never grow in the grass! But they did. They grew there despite what you told me, and now dandelions are everywhere!"

The garden gnome tapped his hollow ceramic head. "Well, that's what you get for listening to a garden gnome."

Fitting In

THE FIRST THING YOU ARE AWARE OF IS SOME-one singing, a woman's voice, first distant and then close as if right beside you.

Rubbish, magical rubbish, popular rubbish—we only want rubbish.
The up! The down! The left! The right!

Now a man joins in. You don't recognize the voices. You don't recognize anything. But the two voices blend together as they sing a second verse.

Rubbish, magical rubbish, popular rubbish—we only love rubbish.
The under! The over! The through and between!

The song repeats; other voices join; other voices leave; but the same two verses are sung again and again of rubbish—rubbish magical and popular. And it is then that you realize you can't see anything. There is the song, and there is darkness, and there is nothing else. Yet you can sense movement around you, and there in the distance, a soft beeping. But where? Who is moving and where is the beeping coming from? What is it?

The darkness recedes as a bright light begins to appear in the center of your vision. Your eyes are closed! That's why it's so dark! You will them to open, but they only move gradually, as if they have forgotten how to move. The bright light grows larger and larger until it reveals itself to be a light in the ceiling above your head, a very blurry light in a very blurry ceiling.

Slowly you turn your head to look to the side. Lights and bottles. Something written on the far wall. A small window by a door, the door open. And through the door a hallway, white tile below a brown desk. There is a woman in the room with you. She is wearing something blue. You look at her face, but all you see is a blur. Somehow you know she is looking at you.

"Awake patient the is!"

Her words seem as blurry as her face.

"Patient is the awake!" the woman calls into the hallway, and soon another person is beside her. Taller. A white jacket. Carrying something. A clipboard? This one is a man. You can tell that much, but his face is as blurry as the woman's.

"When the did patient up wake?" the man's voice asks the woman.

"Now just," the woman answers. "The last within minute."

"Tell sister the patient's," the man says, and the woman leaves the room.

The man is beside your bed, looking closely at you. He shines a flashlight in your eyes. It's bright, much too bright. You raise your hand to deflect it.

"Morning good!" the man says cheerfully. "Good actually afternoon!" he says. "Understand you me can?"

You try to tell him that his words are all jumbled up, but your voice doesn't want to cooperate. The only thing that comes out is a dense mumble of words.

"Rest just for now," the doctor says, putting a hand on your arm. His face has become a little less blurry. You realize there is something different about it, something wrong; but you can't make it out. He turns away and starts writing on his clipboard.

Your attention returns to the wall by the door. Everything is still blurry, but slowly it is becoming more clear. You concentrate your eyes, willing them to focus, and eventually they do. It's your name. That is what is written there. There is a whiteboard on the wall, and someone wrote your name on it.

The doctor is standing above you again. You turn your eyes to him and watch as he continues with his examination. His face isn't blurry anymore. Two streams of grayish-pink liquid are running out of his nose and down his face. A large clump drops off and falls onto your hospital gown. You shout in disgust and push the doctor away.

"Yelling what are you at!" the doctor asks.

A woman clad in blue runs into the room, the same nurse from before, her lower face completely smeared in the grayish-pink stuff that is trickling out of her nose. You shout again.

"Yelling what you are at!" the doctor demands. The nurse is standing by the doctor. Both of their eyes are full of anger.

"Oh, you're awake!" Suddenly, your sister is by your side, hugging you. "I was so worried!"

You turn to her, afraid you'll see the same grayish-pink liquid coming out of her nose, but her face is clean. You let out a sigh of relief.

"Oh, you must be getting cold!" your sister says. She pulls the sheets up over you, just enough to cover the grayish-pink dot on your hospital gown.

"Yelling the patient was," the doctor says. "Why I would like to know."

"It's been three weeks," your sister tells him. "I'm sure it's just the shock of being awake. Isn't that right?"

She turns to you and gives a brief nod of her head, making it clear what your answer is supposed to be.

You look at the doctor and nurse. The grayish-pink liquid is still dribbling out of their noses, but you know you shouldn't yell again. You turn back to your sister, unable to look at the others. "I'm sorry," you manage to force out of your tight throat. "I think I need more rest."

"That's what it is!" your sister says, forcing cheerfulness. "I know I'd be exhausted after sleeping for three whole weeks. Wouldn't you?"

The doctor and nurse share a glance with each other; but, thankfully, they seem satisfied with the answer. From somewhere in the hallway, you can hear the rubbish song.

Rubbish, magical rubbish, popular rubbish—we only want rubbish. The up! The down! The left! The right!

"We will later be back to on you check," the doctor says.

The two of them leave the room, and you turn to your sister and whisper, "What's going on? Why are they leaking stuff out their noses? Why are they talking funny?"

And the possibilities begin to fill your mind. What if you're just seeing and hearing things? What if you're going crazy?

"Is there something wrong with me?" you ask.

Your sister shakes her head and raises a finger to her lips. She stands and walks to the door, which she closes. Then she returns to sit in the chair by your bed.

"No, there's nothing wrong with you, thank goodness. If you were one of them too, I don't know what I'd do."

"One of them?" You glance at the door. It's shut, yet you still lower your voice. "What's going on? Do they really have stuff dripping out of their noses? That's disgusting!"

You look down at the sheet, grateful it is hiding the blob of gunk that dripped out of the doctor's nose onto your hospital gown.

Your sister leans back in her chair. "Do you even know why you're here? Why you've been out for weeks?"

You had completely forgotten about that. The shock of the doctor and nurse had driven the question from your mind. You try to remember what happened.

"I was at work," you say. "And then I went to lunch, and then ... I don't remember."

Your sister nods. "You were in a car accident. That was the day it happened. That was right when it happened."

"When what happened?"

Your sister grasps her ponytail in one hand. She only does that when she is agitated.

"That was the day—no one knows why—half of the world's brains started to melt."

"What? Melt? Their brains started to melt? Half of the world?"

"Well, I guess it's more of a first-world problem," she says. "Not sure why. Maybe it's our cell phones."

She lifts her phone out of her purse and looks at it absently. Then, shrugging, she drops it back in. "But, yeah, their brains started to melt. Right around the time you had your car accident. Maybe the other driver's brain started to melt just then, or maybe he got freaked out when his passenger's brain started to drip out of their nose—"

"Those are brain juices dripping out of their noses?" you ask. You think again of the drop that fell onto your hospital gown. Brain juices! You feel nauseous.

"You can't imagine how crazy it was," your sister says. "Half of the world freaking out about the other half of the world's brains dripping out of their noses, and the other half of the world insisting that their brains weren't dripping out of their noses. No one knew what was going on. Doctors would comment on it at first, but that only lasted for a day or so. The braindrippers hated being told their brains were dripping out of their noses. Just mentioning it was enough to drive them into a rage. Everyone quickly learned to pretend nothing had happened. It was either that or be shunned, so everyone learned to not say anything."

"But they can see our brains aren't dripping out of our noses. Can't they tell we're different?"

"That's okay. They don't care about that. They only care that you pretend *their* brains aren't dripping out of their noses."

"What? But it's disgusting! How can I pretend their brains aren't dripping out of their noses?"

"Actually, that's not the only thing you have to pretend isn't going on."

"There's more?"

"Well, yeah. Their brains are melting. That causes them to do strange things."

"Like what?"

"Well, you heard their talking. It's gotten all jumbled up. And you can hear their rubbish song of course …"

Out in the hallway, you hear multiple voices singing the second verse.

Rubbish, magical rubbish, popular rubbish—we only love rubbish.
The under! The over! The through and between!

"Yeah," you say. "What's up with that? Magical rubbish?"

Your sister shrugs. "I guess they like magic," she says.

"But where did the song come from?"

"No one knows. One day the braindrippers all started singing it, and now that's the only song there is. No one sings anything else anymore."

"But what does the song mean?"

Your sister laughs. "Their brains are melting," she says. "What makes you think it means anything at all?"

"But why are they all singing the same meaningless song?"

"Because their brains are melting!"

You think about it for a moment. It all seems so strange. And everyone is just going along with it? How can people do that? How can they just pretend that people's brains aren't dripping out of their noses?

Out in the hallway, voices are singing about rubbish while other voices speak in jumbled sentences. Yet some of the voices don't sound jumbled you realize, and you see a nurse pass by your window whose nose isn't dripping brain juices.

"I don't get it," you tell your sister. "If only half of the world has melting brains, why are they the ones who are running things?"

"Because the braindrippers control the culture," your sister says, grabbing her ponytail again. "Nine-tenths of the media are braindrippers, so guess what point of view is expressed by the news. And it's not just the media, either. Corporate marketing and human resource departments are full of braindrippers as well, which means that business goes right along with it. And every celebrity is a braindripper—I'm not kidding—every single one of them."

Somehow you aren't surprised.

Your sister continues: "The braindrippers control the culture, which is why they're in charge. And now every song on the radio is the rubbish song. Every soundtrack to every movie and TV show is the rubbish song. Every commercial, every advertisement—rubbish, rubbish, rubbish."

Your conversation is interrupted by a knock at the door. An attendant walks in, carrying a tray of hospital food. There are two thin lines of grayish-pink juice dripping out of the woman's nose.

"Where I should this put?" she asks.

"Just right here," your sister says. She raises your hospital bed into sitting position, and then she extends the foldable table beside the bed over your lap.

The attendant sets the tray down. But, while she is bending over the tray, a drop of brain juice drips off her chin and lands right on top of your chocolate pudding.

Ugh! You cringe, and the attendant notices; but your sister jumps up to save you.

"Thanks!" your sister says and quickly guides the attendant to the door. "I'll make sure it all gets eaten!"

The attendant, who is watching you over her shoulder as she is herded out of the room, says, "The too pudding."

"Of course, that's the best part!" your sister says. Then she closes the door, leaving the two of you alone once more.

You look down at the disgusting grayish-pink goo on top of the chocolate pudding. "There's no way I'm eating that."

"If you don't, you'll be saying that brain juices are dripping out of her nose, and that won't go well," your sister says.

"I don't care. It's not worth it," you say. "It's disgusting! I can't just pretend it's not there!"

"I want you to see something," your sister says. She helps you rise from your bed. Your feet are shaky, but you lean on her as she leads you to the window. "Look down there," she says.

You look out the window at the street below. Cars are passing. Pedestrians are walking back and forth. You think there's something odd about some of them, but you can't put your finger on what it is. "What do you want me to see?" you ask.

"There," your sister says, and she points toward a building across the street where you see a figure huddled in the shadows beside the sidewalk.

At first you think it is a normal panhandler standing there with his hand out. But then you notice how clean and well-kept he looks. That's no ordinary panhandler, you realize. Yet everyone on the street below is taking a wide path around him as if he were a leper. No one will even look at him.

"That person is shunned," your sister says. "He didn't play along. He didn't fit in. Now look what happened to him. When the braindrippers decide you should be shunned, you can say good-bye to your career and your friends. You can say good-bye to everything. I told you: they control the culture. When they say you should be shunned, you're going to be shunned. Is that what you want for yourself?"

Your sister grabs your shoulder and forces you to look at her. "You've got to concentrate on what's important. So what if people's brains are melting? So what if brain juices are dripping out of their noses and they sing a strange song and talk all jumbled up? Do you want to end up like that person down there? That's what's important. That's why you need to always fit in."

You shake your head, disturbed by what you have seen. What has happened to the world? How could it have gone so crazy so fast? Your sister helps you back to the bed. It's amazing how much that little walk to the window has drained you. And you are hungry. You can't believe how hungry you are.

Your sister sits down in the chair next to you again and gets out her phone while you begin to devour your food. It's hospital food, but it's delicious, and you eat everything, everything, that is, but the pudding. No matter how hungry you are, you can't ignore the grayish-pink goo sitting on top of it. You don't care what your sister says. There's no way you're going to eat that.

Your sister gets up and goes into the small bathroom attached to your room. You set down your silverware and lean back on the bed, hoping to process all the craziness your sister has just revealed to you. But as soon as you lean back, the door to your room opens and the attendant returns. She marches over to your bed and examines your tray, immediately noticing you haven't touched the pudding.

"The pudding what's wrong with?" the attendant demands.

"Nothing, I'm just full," you tell her, doing your best to ignore the two streams of grayish-pink brain juices dripping out of her nose.

"The pudding what's with wrong?" the attendant repeats, her voice beginning to rise.

You don't like the look she has in her eyes. "There's nothing wrong with it," you lie. "I just don't feel like pudding right now."

"Pudding what's the wrong with?" the attendant repeats once more. She is almost shouting now, and you know her voice can be heard in the hallway. Will other braindrippers rush in to see what's the matter? Will they all realize why you won't eat the pudding?

Just then the bathroom door bursts open and your sister runs to your side. "Oh, good!" she says. "You saved the pudding for me, just like I asked you to!"

Without hesitation she grabs your spoon and scoops up a big bite, brain juices and all, and stuffs it into her mouth. Your stomach turns at the sight, but your sister acts completely unfazed as she scoops up bite after bite, not stopping until the pudding is completely gone. Then she drops the spoon on the tray, which she hands to the attendant.

"I know it's just hospital pudding," your sister says, "but that's some good stuff." She looks at you expectantly.

The attendant is still glaring, causing you to fumble for words. "I thought you'd like it," you tell your sister. "That's why I was saving it for you."

The attendant looks at you suspiciously, but her glare has lessened. Without another word, she takes the tray and leaves the room. Your sister closes the door behind her and then collapses back into the chair.

"How can you do that?" you ask her. "It was covered in brain juices. That's disgusting!"

Your sister sighs. "I told you. If you refuse to eat something with brain juices on it, then you're saying that their brains are dripping out of their noses, and they hate to be reminded of that. You have to pretend. You have to fit in. The braindrippers are always watching. Every move, every word, every expression. Don't ever forget that. You have to fit in if you don't want to be shunned. You have to do whatever it takes to fit in. Do you understand me?"

"I understand," you tell her. "But that's just so disgusting. I don't know how you can do that."

"There will come a time when you'll be given a choice, when you'll need to decide if you're going to fit in with everyone else or if you're going to accept the consequences."

But you don't want to believe that. Surely there must be some way out of it, you hope. Maybe your sister is wrong. Maybe you'll never have to make that choice.

Thankfully, no more brain juices drip into your food for the remainder of your hospital stay, and three days later the doctors are ready to release you. Your sister is there to check you out of the hospital. She has a large duffel bag, which she sets on the floor and opens.

"Since you wear business casual to work," she says, "I thought it would be good to introduce you to it now. Things have changed a little since people's brains started to melt."

"You mean the styles have changed?"

"You could say that," she says, and she pulls a long-sleeve shirt out of the bag.

"That doesn't look so strange," you start to say, but then she pulls it inside out and puts it on you.

"Why do we wear it like this?" you ask.

"How should I know?" She folds up the long sleeves and pins the ends by your shoulders.

"Why wear long sleeves if you're just going to pin them up anyway?" you ask.

"It's clothing. It's not supposed to make sense. Don't you remember how Dad used to wear baseball hats all the time? Was he playing baseball at the time? No. Did his baseball hat shade his ears? No. Did it shade his neck? No. Yet think of all those men walking around day after day in their baseball hats. Why does that make any sense? Can you think of a more silly hat design for everyone to wear all the time?"

"It just seems like such a waste of time," you say, looking at the pinned-up sleeves.

"Yes, but you're fitting in. That's what counts. We do these pointless, trivial, unnecessary things because everyone else is doing these pointless, trivial, unnecessary things. We're all wasting time together."

She pulls out three socks, a black, a gray, and a white.

"The last time I checked I only have two feet," you say, "and those socks don't even match."

"You're right. They don't," she says. She puts a gray sock on your right foot and a black sock on your left. Then she pulls out some sandals and puts them on your feet.

"Sandals with socks!" you say, feeling completely scandalized.

"How else will everyone know that you're wearing the right color on the right foot?" your sister asks. She pulls out some scissors and cuts the end off the white sock. Then she pulls the cut sock onto your left arm as if it were a medieval gauntlet.

You look at the white sock on your arm. You look down at the black and gray socks on your sandaled feet. "This is crazy!" you say.

"Crazy?" your sister says. "You want to talk about crazy? Well, how about ties? When did those ever make sense? Fashion has always been crazy. We don't notice because we're so used to the craziness. We only notice when it suddenly changes."

And so the next week when you return to work, you wear the inside-out, long-sleeve shirt with the sleeves pinned up, and you wear the black and gray socks with the sandals and you wear the white sock on your left arm. When you walk into the office, you worry you look ridiculous, but as soon as you walk through the doors you see that everyone else looks just as ridiculous, and over time the clothing starts to seem as normal to you as the styles from before.

Like everywhere else, half of your coworkers are braindrippers, and you aren't terribly surprised by which of them have brains dripping out of their noses and which don't. Work continues like it always has before. Things go along as if nothing has changed, but like your sister warned you, the braindrippers are always watching, always watching to make sure you don't squirm at the sight of brain juices dripping out of their noses, always watching to make sure you don't comment on the way their words are jumbled up, or that you don't complain about their constant silly song.

One day a braindripper coworker is leaning over you to look at something on your computer screen, and two drops of brain juices drip down onto the skin of your right arm. You want to scream in disgust. You want to wipe it off frantically. You want to dip your arm in hand sanitizer. But you don't. You just sit there and pretend that nothing has happened. Your coworker lingers by your cubicle for five minutes afterward. Watching, they are always watching. Eventually the braindripper leaves, yet you wait ten more minutes before finally excusing yourself to the bathroom and scrubbing your arm for what seems like forever but doesn't feel nearly long enough.

Yet, day after day you go through the motions. You fit it.

Rubbish, magical rubbish, popular rubbish—we only want rubbish. The up! The down! The left! The right!

When the braindrippers are excited, you are excited. When the braindrippers are upset, you are upset. The reason is rarely clear to you, but reason never matters when you're just trying to fit in.

And things aren't all bad. As time goes by, you discover that the fashion-mandated white sock on your left arm can serve as a useful napkin. No one seems to care how soiled that sock becomes. (Others' socks are often smeared with brain juices.) They only care that you wear it.

And you excel at your work. In the past you might have been an average worker; but now, by virtue of having a non-melting brain, you have become a superior worker. It's no surprise when one day your boss, a braindripper, informs you that you're getting a promotion.

To celebrate, they take you to dinner that night at a fancy steak house you could never have afforded on your own. And there you are, your inside-out, long-sleeve shirt with the sleeves pinned up, and your black and gray socks with sandals, and your white sock on your left arm. And there is everyone else at the table too, wearing the exact same thing, half of them braindrippers, half of them fitting in just like you. You feel proud of yourself at what you have accomplished.

Rubbish, magical rubbish, popular rubbish—we only love rubbish. The under! The over! The through and between!

You try to follow the conversation at your table, but it's difficult given the mixed-up speech of the braindrippers; yet you laugh when everyone laughs, and you scowl when everyone scowls, and you're doing a wonderful job of fitting in until the sparkling water arrives.

The braindripper waiter pours the sparkling water into each glass, one by one. You watch as he makes his way around the table and as the streams of melted brain make their way slowly down his face. When he reaches your glass, you already know what is going to happen. Two large drops of grayish-pink brain juice drip off his chin into your glass, which he sets on the table beside you.

You look at the glass. Everyone at the table looks at you.

"A toast I propose," your boss says. He raises his glass of sparkling water and stands up. Everyone raises their glass as well.

You look at the grayish-pink goo floating in your water. Desperate, you turn and grab the waiter's arm. "I actually didn't want the sparkling water," you tell him. "Could I have a glass of normal water instead?"

"No, toast we'll with sparkling the water," your boss says.

Everyone is holding their glass and staring at you. You lift your glass, and your boss begins his nonsensical toast. You don't listen to his jumbled words. You just watch the brain juices drift around in your glass. Then everyone is clinking their glasses together and drinking, but you don't move. You just sit there, looking at the grayish-pink brain juices swirling slowly.

Above your glass, everyone at the table is staring at you, watching to see what you will do.

Also by Stephen Measure

The River Is Always Waiting

FORCED FROM THEIR cabin seclusion by a mountain storm, Dana and young Alice must accept help from a man Dana had hoped to never see again, a man she no longer trusts—because she knows what darkness calls to him and to what depths he might fall.

Except, let's be blunt—that's not what this book is really about. For too long the world has claimed that attraction is who we are, neglecting to consider the consequences that such logic invites. And society shifts, backs turned against the virtue of resistance, the world afraid to even imagine a man from whom restraint could be expected.

And so, the pleasant wisdom of the past rejected, it's time to use a less comfortable approach. It's time to meet a man the world has been ignoring, time to face him and his story. It's time for us to realize that everyone, absolutely everyone, can choose to resist.

*Attraction is something that you feel,
not something that you are.*

www.ingramcontent.com/pod-product-compliance
Lightning Source LLC
Chambersburg PA
CBHW020100180626
46812CB00006B/2406